Project 314

Bill Burgett

McKenna Publishing Group
Indian Wells, California

Project 314

ISBN: 1-932172-03-3
LCCN: 2002113971

First Edition
10 9 8 7 6 5 4 3 2 1

Visit us on the Web at: www.insomniac.com/mckenna

Printed in the United States of America

This book is dedicated to my twin brother and best friend, Gordon, himself an author and publisher, whose help, guidance, and brotherly love has guided me through the process of getting into print.

1
The River

"It's a bullhead," he said as he gently grabbed it behind its head, being careful not to stick himself with the sharp fins.

"It's a catfish," the older boy argued, laying his pole on the deck of the pier to help his brother.

"Anyone can see it's a bullhead. Look at the tail. It's round. Catfish tails are pointed."

"Who cares, anyway?"

It was a cloudy May morning and the river was swollen from spring rains. The boys had packed potato chips and cokes and brought their fishing poles to the pier. There was an hour to fish before their Dad was to pick them up for Little League, and they intended to catch something before he arrived. Not that they would bring the fish home. No one in their family liked to clean fish, especially their mother, so the bluegills, bullheads, and catfish would be thrown back after sufficient bragging time.

"There's sure a lot of stuff in the river," said the older boy. He was in the eighth grade, about to start high school. "Must be over its banks upriver to pick up so many branches and stuff." He could see that the water was halfway up the boat ramp.

The younger boy was in the sixth grade and would be going to middle school. He was busy trying to get his hook out of the bullhead. The fish had swallowed the hook. With only two in his box, the boy wanted to save the hook, but didn't want to gut the fish. He decided in favor of the hook and gave a sharp pull on the line. Out came the hook and stringy pieces of fish gut. Blood dripped on the boy's pants. "What should I do with it?" he asked. "I think I've killed it."

"Throw it back. Something'll eat it." The older boy was busy putting a fresh worm on his hook. Neither boy saw the hand bobbing up and down in rhythm with the current. It was sticking out from between branches under the short pier next to the boat ramp. They were seated on worn wooden benches on top of the pier. A waist-high railing ran the length of the pier. Notches had been cut in the top rail to keep fishing poles from sliding away.

The older brother raised his pole overhead and gently cast bobber, sinker, and hook about ten feet away from the pier. The sinker pulled the wiggling worm under the water and immediately the whole rig was carried in the direction of the current. The bobber kept everything off the bottom. The boy's eyes were glued to the bobber.

The younger boy sent the disemboweled bullhead into the current with a twinge of guilt. He hated to hold worms, but he knew that his older brother would call him names if he didn't, so he reached into the cardboard container and pulled a worm out of the clump, then threaded his hook through it. He cast his rig over the rail and the current pulled it under the pier. He felt an instant tug. "I've got another one!" he called out. "It's huge! Get the net."

The older boy reeled in his rig and went for the net. "Let out some line before the fish breaks it," he yelled. While his brother held the pole, the older boy went behind the pier and got down on his knees and tried to reach the line. Instead he grabbed what felt like a rag. He pulled on it until he could see what he had in his hands. His hands sprang open as if he had grabbed a hot coal. "It's a leg!" he screamed. "It's somebody's leg!"

The younger boy dropped his pole and ran to the far end of the pier. At the same time their father pulled into the turnaround at the head of the boat ramp and honked his horn. Both boys ran to the car with looks of terror on their faces. "There's a dead body under the pier," the older boy screamed as if his father was hearing impaired. The father parked the car and walked quickly to the pier with his oldest son while the sixth-grader stayed behind. It was clear that the body wasn't going anywhere so the father decided not to touch it. He called 911 from his cell phone.

Within minutes sirens came from every direction. Three police cars and a rescue squad squeezed into the turnaround. Radios were blaring. Lights were flashing. Men started pulling on waders behind the rescue squad.

Two hours later, the police released the boys and their father and drove away from the pier with the body of what appeared to be a middle-aged man in a body bag. Yellow police tape was strung around the ramp and the pier. The boys put their fishing poles in their father's car and began to rehearse the story they would tell their mother.

Riverside didn't grow like other bedroom communities close to the city. Part of the reason was the river. It divided the town in half and there were only two car bridges and the railroad bridge. The town was old and pleased with its history.

What it lacked in size it made up in wealth. Most of the houses were built on spacious well-maintained lots. As the city had grown, the town of Riverside had become a great place for commuters who wanted to live the small-town life.

Sergeant Mark Garrison, a Riverside native, was one of seven employees in the Police Department. Much of his boyhood had been spent catching bull-heads where the boys had found the body. His initials were carved into the railing at the pier. MG and KL were carved inside a heart. Mark had thought of Kay when he was at the river the day before. It had been a long time since he had been to the pier. As a boy, Mark thought of his childhood sweetheart as the girl he would eventually marry. It never happened. Kay's father moved the family away when Mark and Kay were in the eighth grade and they had since lost contact. After Riverside High, Mark enlisted in the Army and became a military policeman. Military life wasn't for Mark, however. His heart never left Riverside. Discharged honorably after three years, he returned and was imme-diately hired by the Riverside Police Department as an officer. When he earned his Associate's Degree in Law Enforcement at the Community College, he was promoted to sergeant. With twelve years experience, he would be eligible for promotion to Lieutenant when an opening occurred. Well-groomed, with his hair cut military-style, Mark took his police work seriously. He had an infec-tious smile that came easily to his square-jawed face. He could feel his biologi-cal clock ticking at thirty-six and, like his father, there was already some gray in his dark hair. Because he disliked writing notes, he carried a pocket tape re-corder wherever he went. Sue, the Riverside Police clerk, transposed his tapes in her spare time as a courtesy. Mark knew that if Sue ever left the department, he'd be up the creek.

Riverside was a law-abiding town. Major crime consisted of car break-ins and family disputes. Bodily injury was rare except at the Corner Pub on occa-sional Friday or Saturday nights. Mark was responsible for day-to-day police matters and had three officers reporting to him. He reported to Lieutenant Corcoran who in turn reported to Captain Myers. In addition to six policemen, there was one clerk. The mechanic at Stan's Exxon station maintained the department's three patrol cars and Mark's unmarked car, and calibrated the ra-dar units.

The buzz at the station was about the dead body pulled out of the river. Mark and two other officers had responded to the 911 call. A rescue squad from the volunteer fire department had also responded. "What's the story on

the floater?" Sue asked as Mark came through the door with a bag of Dunkin'
Donuts.

"Don't know much yet," he replied. "The squad took him to the clinic.
Doctor Spencer will examine him this morning. Here's my tape. You'll know
everything I know when you type the report," he said with a smile.

Doctor Spencer was a retired physician who had delivered just about every
baby born in Riverside for the past thirty-six years. Although retired from practice, he was still the town coroner. His specialty was family medicine. He had
served the town as coroner for as long as he could remember, charging for his
services by the hour. The clinic served as the town's first-aid facility since it was
built. It was as close to a hospital as you could get in Riverside. Under new
HMO ownership a same-day surgery wing had been added.

Dr. Spencer had the body taken to the new wing where he did his examina-
tion. Not being a surgeon, he didn't plan to do a full autopsy. The cause of
death was apparent—drowning or shooting, depending on whether the bullet
killed the man before he went into the river. Examining the contents of the
lungs would help make that decision. There were no other suspicious marks on
the body. The man was dressed in casual clothes—a long-sleeved blue shirt
and dark cotton pants, walking shoes and ankle-length socks. His pockets were
empty. The condition of the body suggested that he had been in the water less
than two days. A bullet entered his head at the right temple and exited through
the left eye. The entry and exit holes were small, probably from a .22 caliber
handgun. Spencer didn't check for powder evidence since the body was im-
mersed for several days.

Spencer determined the man to be in his late thirties, balding in the temple
areas, measuring 5'11" and weighing 173 lbs. He appeared to have been healthy,
but not particularly muscular. What was left of his face had not been shaved
for several days. There was a scar on the top of his right wrist where a bone
fusion had been done, probably as a result of an injury to the wrist. Otherwise
his condition was unexceptional. His lungs were filled with river water suggesting that he entered the river alive. Considering the lack of bruising, abrasions,
or other injuries to the body, Spencer considered the death to be caused by a
self-inflicted gunshot wound and subsequent drowning. He assumed the man
had positioned himself to fall into the river, then shot himself in the temple
with a small caliber handgun, or had shot himself in the temple after entering
the river. Spencer saw no need to take further action and released the body to
Mueller's Funeral Home to be held pending identification.

After cleaning up, the doctor drove to the police station and gave his report to Sue since he no longer had secretarial privileges at the clinic. Sue dropped what she was doing and typed the report. Spencer came by after lunch, corrected some spelling, signed the report, and took it to Captain Jeff Myers.

"What's your opinion, Doctor?" asked the Captain.

"It's in the report, Jeff," he said. "I believe it's open and shut—a suicide. What I can't tell you is why he did it or who he is."

"Never seen him?" Jeff knew that there was no one in Riverside who had not been examined by Dr. Spencer. If Dr. Spencer didn't know the man, he was from the outside for sure.

"Never," Spencer replied.

Jeff accepted the Doctor's conclusion. He called through the open door, "Get Mark in here, Sue." Spencer left and Mark came in.

"Hi, Doc, had an exciting morning?" Mark asked as he passed Dr. Spencer in the doorway.

"When you're retired, Mark, it doesn't take a lot to perk up a day. Good luck."

"What do you think, Jeff? Is the Doc right?" Mark asked.

"I think so. I'd like to know where, when, and why before I put a lid on this, though. So far nothing is showing up on missing persons from Riverside or the city or the state. I'd like you to handle this one, Mark. Can't spare any help for you. Any questions?"

"I'll let you know."

Life moved on in Riverside. The Herald moved the story to an inside page. The yellow police tape at the pier was the only reminder that a body had been found. It was there that Mark began his investigation. Knowing that the river was still high, Mark threw work boots in the trunk of his unmarked police car. His first objective would be to find the gun, but he would need to know where the man entered the river. If Dr. Spencer and Jeff were right about the man shooting himself, the gun couldn't be far from the point that he entered the river. The question was how far did the body travel before it came to rest under the pier? Could he have killed himself at the pier? It would have been a convenient place to get into the river. For that matter, why would a man need to go into the river if he was going to shoot himself? Why not just shoot himself? But that wouldn't dispose of a body. Maybe he wanted to disappear, but why? What difference would it make after he was dead? Maybe he had a family that he didn't want to see him with a bullet hole in his head. Maybe it wasn't a suicide after all. The gun would be the key. If he found the gun, it could still be printed, even if it were submerged. If it was a suicide the prints could not have been wiped off. He had to find the gun. If a man shot himself in the head, the gun would have fallen from his hand where he stood.

Ed Braun would be the man to see. Ed had lived his whole life in Riverside. Injured in a track meet in high school, Ed was unable to do hard physical work. He still lived in his parent's home. When they died, he stayed on. He received a small check from the government each month and helped out at the train station for extra money. But most of his time was spent at the river. He loved to fish and knew every inch of the riverbank near Riverside. Everyone in town knew Ed. He had put worms on every kid's hook, taught scouts and others how to tell fish apart and what bait to use. He was the man who could tell Mark how far that body could have traveled in the river.

Mark found Ed where he expected to find him—in a booth at Marge's. "Hi, Marge," he called out as he slid into Ed's booth.

"Anything, Mark?" she called from behind the counter. Marge had run the old diner since her husband died of a stroke at the age of thirty-two. If you wanted to know what was happening in Riverside, the diner was the place to be. Small groups of locals gathered there every morning, noon, and evening for catching up and Marge's home-cooked meals. Cracks were beginning to appear in the vinyl upholstery in the booths. Marge had considered redecorating, but couldn't afford anything elaborate. Anyway, she was getting on in years. Maybe it was time to retire.

"Coffee. Black. And corned beef hash with toast." He turned to Ed. Ed looked great. He was clean-shaven and wearing a new red plaid flannel shirt and clean jeans. Mark couldn't remember seeing Ed in anything but jeans. Mark had always envied Ed's easy lifestyle. "How are you doing, Ed?"

"Okay, Mark. Actually, I'm killing some time. Nothing going on at the station this morning. What's up?"

"You read about the body we found at the pier?"

"Yep. Do you know who it was?"

"Not yet. And no one seems to care. No missing report yet, but Jeff has me on the case. I need your help, Ed."

"I'll do what I can. How do you think I can help?"

"The body was tangled in some branches under the pier when the boys found it. We think the man shot himself, but we don't know how or where he got into the water. I thought you might have some ideas. I need to find the gun to know whether it was a suicide or a homicide."

"How long does Doc Spencer think he was dead when the boys found him?"

"No more than two days. There was little decomposition."

"That would mean that he died on Thursday or Friday. It rained on Thursday. The water was already up from all the rain we've had this spring and the river was moving pretty good. This river is deep. If he went in near the middle, he could have been carried any distance by the current. If he went in off the bank, he wouldn't have drifted far because of all the fallen trees and branches at the edge. The only way for him to go in at the middle would be off one of the bridges. That's not likely. Center St. bridge has no walkway. Ellinwood St. Bridge has a walkway, but it's on the other side of town. He couldn't have drifted that far. The railroad bridge would be the only possibility, but a person would be pretty desperate to climb up onto the railroad bridge."

"Suicide is desperate."

"Let's assume that he fell off the railroad bridge after he shot himself. The current would have carried him about a quarter of a mile. If that were true, his body would have drifted to the bend at the pier. The pier would have stopped it because of the clutter underneath. My guess would be that he went in at the railroad bridge. I'd start there. Bet you'll find your gun on the bridge."

Ed finished his breakfast, but waited while Mark finished his corned beef hash and coffee. Mark paid for both meals. "Thanks, Ed. I'll let you know what I find."

There were two ways to get to the top of the railroad bridge. Starting at the base of the bridge one could climb a steep incline up a gravel hill to the bridge, a climb of approximately thirty feet. Or one could hike about a quarter mile along the tracks from the railroad station. Mark opted for the latter. There weren't many trains that came through town anymore and there was walking room at the side of the tracks if a train did come. He went to the trunk of his unmarked police car and put on his boots. It took about fifteen minutes to get to the bridge. He remembered all the times as a boy that he had stood on the railroad bridge. His parents warned against it, but the temptation was just too great for a boy. This time was different.

Ed was right. A Phoenix HP-22 was in the gravel near the place where the bridge crossed the center of the river. The man could have shot himself while standing on the bridge, then fallen over the knee-high railing at the edge of the bridge. From there he would have fallen into the middle of the river, just as Ed thought. Mark found a stick and ran it up the barrel of the pistol, then dropped it into a plastic bag. Mark loved life. He couldn't imagine what demons could drive a man to kill himself.

"Got the gun," Mark announced as he walked into the station. Sue looked up as he passed by and watched him walk into the Lieutenant's office. "Where's Corky?" he asked.

"He's out," Sue replied. Lieutenant Corcoran was seldom in the office. Mark found Jeff sitting in the small room that served as a closet and break room.

"Got the gun," he repeated as he lifted the bag to show it to Jeff. "If it's got prints, we might be able to identify the body."

"Take it to the city lab," Jeff said. "I don't want us to do it here. The serrated handle will make it tricky."

"If I leave now I'll be able to get it to the lab and get back before the city is in gridlock," Mark replied.

"Let me know when you get the results," Jeff asked.

On his way out of the station, Mark dropped two microcassettes on Sue's desk without saying a word. She ignored the gift.

2
Missing Person

Judy could hear the phone ringing as she finished paying the taxi driver. She knew she wouldn't get to the phone before the machine took the call so she didn't rush, although she was eager to hear the messages. She hadn't heard from Bob since Thursday.

As she opened the door her Welsh Corgi, Kelly, greeted her with his usual dribble on the rug. He ignored the infraction and barked enthusiastically. She dropped her weekender and cosmetic bag in the front hallway of their rehabilitated townhouse and headed straight for the phone. There were five messages. She was pleased. Maybe Bob had stayed downtown while she was away and had left a message for her. She hit the "play" button. The first two messages were hang-ups—probably marketing calls. She hated those. The third and fourth were her own messages to Bob. The last message was from her mother. She dialed her mother's number. After some openers she said, "It's not like him not to call. There were no messages at the hotel and there is nothing on the answering machine. He may have stayed at the lab while I was away. He's been doing that more and more lately, but he's good about calling everyday. He's been so distracted lately. I don't know what to make of it."

"Don't worry, Judy. Why don't you call him now at the lab? I'll talk to you later. I love you."

Knowing how much Bob hated to be disturbed at the lab she decided to pour a glass of wine and get settled. It was good to be home. The yearly teacher's conferences were enjoyable, especially getting caught up on the latest gossip with her former classmates, and she was now done with her CEU's for the year.

The townhouse was always welcoming. Built in the early twenties, it had been recycled through good times and bad. Bob and Judy had spent more than they could afford getting it restored, but now it would do the original owners proud. No more paint on the woodwork or window frames. No more worn carpets over hardwood floors. No more painted wallpaper on plaster walls. No more cheap linoleum in the kitchen and bathrooms. Everything was restored.

The townhouse was three stories, counting the basement. The first floor included a large living room, a formal dining room, and a kitchen with a large walk-in pantry. There was no bathroom on the first floor. The second floor included three bedrooms and one hallway bathroom with a lion's paw tub. Each bedroom had a small closet. Bob and Judy had chosen the front bedroom, even though it was over the street and the loudest of the three, because it had a walkout balcony with double French doors.

In the kitchen she poured herself a glass of white port and carried it to the bedroom. Bob liked her in tee shirts, so she kicked off her shoes and traded her blouse and skirt for a pair of jeans and a clingy tee shirt. No one answered the phone at the lab.

Judy wasn't the worrying type. As a high school teacher, she had learned to deal with just about everything imaginable, but this uneasy feeling about Bob's silence wouldn't go away. He had her agenda. He knew she'd be home today. Surely, he'd be coming through the doors any time. She'd wait it out.

It felt good to sit on the NordicRider and stretch her muscles. Three hours in coach seats had made her stiff. Judy had healthy habits—no drugs, occasional wine, lots of exercise and early to bed. Used to taking care of herself, and conscious of her appearance, she had not felt the effects of the mid-thirties. Some of her friends were starting to wrinkle and sag. At 126 lbs. and 5'7", she could pass for a much younger woman. Because Bob liked long blonde hair, she had hers cut just below her shoulder line. Being cross-brained, she could hold her own with a budget or a guitar. Her only vice was quiz shows. Twice she had tried to get on Jeopardy, but failed. If she couldn't watch the show, she taped it.

Bob and Judy deferred children. Unless Bob's hours changed, that would be a permanent decision for Judy. No way would she bring a child into a fatherless family, but she didn't like to think about going through life childless. His workaholism was stressing their relationship. Something would have to give and she didn't look forward to another confrontation with Bob, at least today.

Kelly finally made it up the stairs and lay down next to the NordicRider. His short legs and old age made it difficult for him to climb the high stairs to the second floor. Judy stopped exercising and sat on the floor with Kelly for a long time. She didn't know why, but she began to cry.

After a while, she closed the blinds, took off all her clothes and began to unpack. Judy seldom wore any clothes when she was home alone. She never quite reconciled the freedom of nudity with her faith life. An active member of her church and regular student in the adult Bible class, she never missed worship and went twice a week during Advent and Lent.

When Bob didn't return by dinnertime, Judy fixed herself a salad and ate it alone. The lab was only three miles from their townhouse. Her well-worn Ford Escort was parked on the street in front of the townhouse. After getting dressed she drove to the lab but never got out of the car. From the street she could see that there were no lights burning in the lab. She decided to call around. Something was very wrong.

When she got home she went straight to the phone. Bob was a loner. He had few close personal friends. His parents and brother had not heard from him. Finally, she called Bev Hudson, his lab partner. Bev had seen Bob on Thursday, but he didn't come in to the lab on Friday. She didn't think anything of it since Bob had been making regular business trips on Fridays. "Is anything wrong?" asked Bev.

"I haven't heard from Bob since I left for Chicago on Thursday, and he wasn't at home when I got back. It's not like him," Judy replied.

"Have you called the hospitals, Judy?"

"No, that's next, I guess. Thanks, Bev."

"Let me know if I can help."

"Thanks. I will."

There were only two hospitals in their end of the city. Neither had admitted a Bob Archer. Calling the police was another option, but it seemed too radical at the moment.

Judy knew when she went to bed that it would be a long night. At 11:30 she was still wide-awake. "This is nuts. Something's wrong. I'm going to the police," she muttered to herself as she reached for the lamp. After slipping into her bathrobe and slippers, she splashed some water on her face. Her jeans and tee shirt were lying over the back of the rocker where she had left them. Kelly kept sleeping on the floor at the foot of the bed. Judy loved the dog, but she drew the line at letting him sleep on the bed.

After turning out the lights in the bedroom and quietly slipping out of the house, she remembered that she didn't have a clue as to where the police department was located. She went back in and checked the blue section of the Yellow Pages. There was a police station near her townhouse.

Luckily, there was a parking place in front of the station, an old stone-on-stone building. The steel and glass high-security doors looked out of place on the stately old building. The outer door led to a small vestibule, which then offered a choice of doors at either side—one of which led to a large room divided by a chest-high counter. A sign on the door read "Public Entrance." Judy pushed her way in. Behind the counter was a fifty-something uniformed policeman. He looked attentive but idle. A small radio behind him was playing elevator music. Another stack of electronic equipment was shotgunning radio calls. Judy wondered how anyone could understand what was being said. No one else was in sight and the offices behind the counter were dark. "How can I help you?" he asked with a sincere tone and a friendly smile. His inventory of her physical assets didn't go unnoticed.

"I haven't heard from my husband since Thursday," she said. "It isn't like him. I think something is wrong."

"Are you reporting a missing person?"

"Yes. His name is Bob Archer."

He stepped away from the counter and went into an office behind the counter. When he came back, he said, "No department reports since Thursday on a Bob Archer. Sorry. And I don't have a clerk here to take your report. There will be someone here at 6:00. Can you come back then?"

"Okay." A little confused, she turned to go.

"By the way," he said in a raised voice. "It would help if you could bring a picture of your husband when you come. And I wouldn't worry, Miss. They usually turn up on their own."

Judy knew what he was thinking, but by this time Judy was convinced that something was very wrong. Her imagination began to work overtime. As she drove back to the townhouse, she began to consider the possibilities. Maybe Bob was tired of the confrontations, too. Maybe he had left her, but he hadn't taken anything—not even his toothbrush. Maybe he had been called to D.C. again, but no note? That's not Bob. Maybe he had—she didn't want to go on. Things like that didn't happen to them. She was getting too dramatic. Still, something was wrong.

Kelly was inside barking when Judy walked up to the door. She opened the door, entered her security code, and took Kelly out on the leash. On her way back in she passed by the stately grandfather clock in the front hallway and noticed that it was already 2:00. The chimes had been quieted long ago because they kept Bob awake. There was no point trying to sleep since she had to be at the police station at 6:00. In the kitchen she fixed a cup of black coffee and filled Kelly's water bowl. He had plenty of dry food. She called in to the school office and left a message on the answering machine that she would not be in.

They would need a substitute. It was the first day she had missed in the school year. No one could complain. She didn't give a reason. None was necessary. She had accumulated plenty of paid personal days. Then she remembered the officer's request for a picture.

Normally, Judy was a neatnic. But when it came to pictures, except for those in deco frames, she had never taken the time to organize albums. All the photos of a lifetime, except for the wedding pictures, were thrown into a big cardboard box on the top shelf of the rear bedroom closet. Judy got the box down and plopped it on the floor beside the rocker in her bedroom. She turned on the floor lamp and reached into the box for a handful of photos.

Kelly barked when the newspaper slammed against the front door. Judy snapped to attention. Her neck ached. She had fallen asleep with her head tilted back on an Afghan drooped over the back of her rocker. On the floor were piles of photographs. She must have fallen asleep while going through the pictures. The sun was up. What time was it? The red numbers on the dresser clock/radio said 6:20. She picked up a photo of Bob standing by his Taurus, then thought that they would probably want a portrait. The only portrait she had was on the dresser, so she took it out of the frame and headed for the bathroom. After freshening herself, she took Kelly out on the leash, then headed for the police department.

A different officer greeted her. The station had come alive. There were lights on in all the offices. He picked up the phone and spoke to someone named Carol. Soon a young woman in civilian clothes came out and introduced herself. "I'm Carol. Will you come with me, please?" Judy was led to a small desk in a room filled with cluttered desks. No one else was present. Carol pointed to a wooden chair at the side of the desk. Judy sat down wondering how many others had sat in that chair and what stories they had told.

"You were here earlier, I understand," Carol said. "Could you fill me in, please?" Her fingers were poised over a keyboard and she was gazing into a monitor. "Why don't we start with your name?"

Judy told her about Bob and gave the necessary details.

"May I have the picture you brought? I'll make a copy and give you the original before you leave. I'm going to need a lot more information about your husband. Would you like a cup of coffee before we start?"

It dawned on Judy that she hadn't eaten anything since her salad the previous afternoon. "Yes, with a little cream, please."

Carol brought coffee, cream, and a plain donut on a paper plate. "Let's start with some biographical details about your husband. When and where was he born?"

"June 17, 1963. Chicago."

"Does he still look like this?" she asked nodding toward the portrait.

"He's balding at the temples and getting a 'monk's cap.' There's a scar on his right wrist from hand surgery. He's 5'11" and weighs about 175 undressed, with hazel eyes and brown hair. His health is good."

"Please understand, Mrs. Archer. I have to ask the following questions," Carol apologized in advance. "Are you getting along with your husband?"

"Like any other couple, I guess. We have some issues, but, yes, we're getting along."

"Is one of those 'issues' another woman? Sorry, but it's important information in missing person's cases."

"No. He doesn't have enough time for me. His 'mistress' is his work."

"What kind of work?"

"He's a scientist. He has a Ph.D. and M.D. and works at a biological laboratory here in the city. They do contract work for the Human Genome Project. He doesn't talk much about it."

"Does he have any other interests? Sorry, again, but is he compulsive about anything—drinking, gambling or things like that?"

"Just work. He likes music, especially country western. He is a great acoustic guitarist. Occasionally we go line dancing. That's about it."

"Last question. What kind of car does he drive?"

"A 1995 Ford Taurus—blue."

"Where is it now?"

"I don't know. It's with him, I guess."

"Where can we reach you if we have to?"

"I'll be home today. After that, I don't know. I'll call you tomorrow with my plans."

"I wouldn't worry, Mrs. Archer. These things have a way of working out."

Judy wasn't consoled, and she wasn't offended by another pat answer. These people had heard it all. She drove home by way of Denny's where she got a full breakfast, then a hot shower, and dozed by the phone.

3
Suicide?

Mark was sitting at his desk when Sue approached. "Mueller's called. They want to know how long they're supposed to keep the floater?"

"Sue, please don't call him 'the floater.' It sounds so disrespectful."

"Sorry. I heard it on Law and Order. Anyway, Dr. Spencer also called about identifying the body. He wants you to call him. What should I tell Mueller's?"

"Tell them it shouldn't be much longer." Mark dialed Dr. Spencer's number.

"Hello, Dr. Spencer here."

Mark was afraid he had awakened the doctor. "Hi. Mark Garrison. I'm returning your call. Hope I didn't call too early."

"No, it's fine. Mark, have you ID'd the body yet?"

"Not yet. We're working on it."

"I didn't do prints or dentals the other day. Do you want me to go down to Mueller's for more information?"

"Yes."

"I'll get back to you."

"Thanks, Doc. Sue, have you finished my tapes yet?" Mark called from his desk.

"I'm working on them."

"Thanks. When you're done, will you call downtown and see if they have anything on the gun."

"Okay."

Mark was trying to put the pieces of the puzzle together. He looked into his coffee mug as he thought about the man whose life had ended in his little town. The mug was brown with coffee stains. Although his mind was elsewhere, his legs took him to the break room where he poured hot water and a squirt of liquid hand soap into his mug, then let it soak on the side of the sink. On his way back to his desk he heard his phone ring. "Who is it, Sue?" he asked.

"It's Ed Braun. Something about a car at the railroad station."

"Hey, Ed."

"Mark, there's a Taurus that's been down here for awhile. Could you check the plates for me?"

"Sure, Ed. I'll have Sue call you. Where will you be?"

"Leave a message on the machine at the station."

"Will do."

Five parking spots on Laurel Street were designated "Reserved for Passengers—24-hour limit". Passengers who spent the night in the city used these. Occasionally a passenger made arrangements with Ed to stay extra days. Ed tagged those cars so they wouldn't get cited. The Taurus had been there for several days without a tag. Ed wasn't sure when it first showed up. He gave Mark the license number.

"Sue, run these tags will you and let me know?"

"Sure, Mark."

Five minutes later Sue buzzed Mark on his phone. "The tags are registered to a Dr. Bob Archer. He has a city address. It has not been reported stolen. Want me to call Veterans?"

"Not yet. See if you can raise Ed Braun. I'd like to talk to him first."

"Done deal."

The hand soap had done its job. Weeks of coffee grime rinsed out of Mark's cup. He poured fresh coffee into his revitalized mug, grabbed a donut, and headed back to his desk. *I've got to eat better,* he thought. Sue approached him as he made the turn into his office.

"Ed's on the line. When you're done with him, buzz me. I just got the report on the prints. You won't believe what I've got."

Mark took Ed's call at Sue's desk. "Ed, the car isn't hot. It belongs to some doctor in the city. Is it a problem to give him a few more days?"

"No, there are only two cars in the station parking spaces."

"Okay. Let's give him a break. If it isn't gone by Thursday, call Veterans." Veterans was the only towing service in Riverside. They were willing to pick up unauthorized cars and charge the owners.

"If you say so, Mark."

While Mark was waiting for Sue to return to her desk, he noticed the lab report, picked it up and read the brief summary. He couldn't believe what he saw. The mystery was solved. The dead man was Dr. Bob Archer. According to the lab, the prints on the handgun were those of Dr. Bob Archer. The match was made with prints taken for a security clearance. Although partial, they were sufficient to run an ID. No other prints were found on the gun and no attempt had been made to remove the prints. The prints were right hand prints meaning that Archer had held the gun in his right hand, which was consistent with a right temple entry wound. The gun could be picked up at any time.

"I told you you'd be surprised," Sue said as she slipped behind her desk. Sometimes Sue was like a teenager when things got interesting. She loved police work. Her father was retired from the city force and had instilled a high respect for police work in his family.

"More relieved than surprised," said Mark. "I knew we'd ID the guy eventually, but now what? Call Ed, Sue, and tell him not to touch the car. I mean that literally—don't even put a hand on the car. We'll be down to go over it this afternoon, then we'll call Veterans."

Mark went into Jeff's office. "We have an ID on the body. It seems he parked by the railroad station. We have his car and have chased the tags. The same guy's prints are on the gun. He's a doctor named Bob Archer. He apparently parked in the station lot, walked to the railroad bridge, shot himself and fell into the river."

"Or was met at the station, taken to the bridge and shot."

"I don't think so, Jeff. There are no other prints on the gun. Right hand prints are consistent with a right-hand entry wound. I think Dr. Spencer is right. It adds up to suicide."

"If I made what doctors make these days, I wouldn't shoot myself."

"Maybe he wasn't that kind of doctor. Could have been a Ph.D."

"Let's find out. Stay on it, Mark. Chase down the good doctor."

"I've got to go into the city and get the gun. Dr. Archer lived in the city. I'll see what I can dig up. What about Mueller's?"

"Tell them we've got an ID. We'll let them know as soon as we've talked to the family."

Sue rushed into Jeff's office and uncharacteristically interrupted Mark and Jeff. "Sorry to interrupt you, but I have more news on the floater, I mean Dr. Archer. Look at what just showed up on the fax machine."

It was clearly Dr. Bob Archer day at the Riverside police station. A missing person's report had been faxed from the city police. The name of the missing person was Bob Archer. "The picture looks similar to the body," Mark offered.

"A few days in the river is not good for the complexion," quipped Jeff. Mark hoped that he would never become flippant about human life. He excused Jeff and wrote it off to his many years in police work.

"Mark, when you pick up the gun, talk about jurisdiction. I'd like to get to the bottom of this one. Anyway, it gives us practice. If we keep jurisdiction, locate the family and break the news, okay?"

"Thanks, Jeff. Sure that isn't the chief's job?"

It was already ten and Mark's day was a disaster. He wanted to get to the Taurus before going to the city, but he also wanted to avoid the late afternoon traffic gridlock. "Sue, call Don Huber on his cell phone," he asked. "Have him get prints from the car." Huber was the only town officer who had fingerprinting experience.

Sue got lucky. Huber was on his way back to the station. "He'll be in your office in about ten minutes," Sue said as she hung up the phone.

Mark wasn't sure whether they would get the case. Archer lived in the city and worked in the city. On the other hand, Mueller's had the body, and the crime, if it was a crime, had occurred in Riverside. Mark had a good case for claiming jurisdiction. Anyway, no charges would be pressed if Jeff could be convinced that the death was a suicide. It would just be a matter of paperwork.

Don Huber was a new officer. He had earned an associate degree in law enforcement, then breezed through the police academy where he had taken an extra course on the latest fingerprinting techniques. That made him the department expert. "What's up, Mark," he asked as he strolled toward Mark's office. He was 6'7" tall and weighed 235 lbs. and he was all muscle from playing basketball and lifting weights. Everyone felt secure in his company.

"We've got a Taurus at the railroad station that belonged to the man you printed for Doc Spencer at Mueller's. Spencer thinks the death is a suicide and I'm inclined to agree, but I want to check the Taurus to be sure there isn't anything unusual. Can you go over there with me now?"

"Yes, but I have to make a call first," Don replied.

The car was locked, but Ed Braun had opened many stranded cars over the years for Veterans. He slipped his stick into the door well and was in the car in a minute, being careful not to touch the door handles. Don lifted prints from the front door handles, steering wheel, gearshift knob and radio button while Mark rifled the glove compartment and the trunk. The contents of the glove compartment were typical: owner's manual, registration, two maps, paper napkins, toothpicks, and lifesavers. The trunk was empty except for tire changing equipment in a special compartment. It appeared as though the trunk had never been used. Nothing was found under the seats.

"Hold the car until I call you, Ed. It will probably be tomorrow. I doubt that we'll impound it," Mark called out as they were pulling away.

Don Huber was dropped off at the station with instructions to call Mark on his cell phone if any print other than Bob Archer's showed up. Mark headed for the city.

Carol's name was on the missing report fax, so when Mark got to the police station he asked for her. "We've got your Bob Archer," he said. "He's the body we fished out of the river over the weekend."

"Great," she said in a tone that suggested a problem. "I was the one who took the report from his wife. I told her not to worry. I feel sorry for her."

"I need to talk to the charge officer. We want jurisdiction. Can you take me to him?" Mark asked.

"Her," said Carol. "It's Captain Louise Gordon. Follow me, and good luck."

Captain Gordon was the first female captain in the history of the precinct. She had weathered the transition, but the experience had hardened her. A divorcee, she pursued police work when her husband left her a single mother with two kids. Her timing was perfect. There were only seven female officers on the force when it opted for inclusiveness. Six of the seven received rapid promotions. Gordon was the first to make captain, a move resented by many male veterans. Gordon was in a conference with two police officers when Carol tapped on the window of her office door. She opened the door a crack. "Yes?"

"I have a gentlemen here who needs to talk with you," Carol announced.

"We're done here. Come on in."

Mark introduced himself and extended his hand.

Louise Gordon did not extend the courtesy. "Sit down," she ordered.

Mark told her the story about Archer and suggested that they discuss jurisdiction. The surly captain had no interest in Archer or his case. "He's yours," she said. "We've got all we can handle."

"I'll need the missing persons file."

Captain Gordon pointed Mark to Carol. He rose, but didn't extend his hand. Gordon remained seated and didn't acknowledge his departure.

"She's a piece of work," Carol said to Mark as they walked to the front door. "But don't let her bother you. She's that way to everyone. It's great for morale. Good luck with Mrs. Archer. I don't envy your job."

Mark left with the missing person's file and mixed feelings. Getting jurisdiction was easy, now came the hard part. He checked the file for the Archer address, then headed for their townhouse. On the way, he passed a Burger King and grabbed a Whopper and shake.

4
The Funeral

Judy Archer was tired after a sleepless night. Staying home from school, she waited for some word about Bob. The police department was patient with her, but she was pushing her luck and didn't want to make another call just to hear again that they were working on the case, but there was nothing new. Kelly barked furiously when Mark knocked on the leaded glass window in the front door. The dog followed Judy down the stairs and wagged his tail at the prospect of a visitor. Mark usually wore civilian clothes and always drove an unmarked vehicle, so it was not apparent that he was a police officer. Being alone, Judy was hesitant to invite him in. She opened the door as far as the chain would allow. "Yes?" she greeted.

"Mrs. Archer?"

"Yes, what can I do for you?" She was apprehensive.

"I'm Sergeant Garrison," Mark said as he held his police badge up to the door. "I need to talk to you about Dr. Archer. May I come in?"

Judy's eyes were flooding with tears when Mark came into the hallway. Her heart was pounding and her knees seemed as though they would buckle at any minute. She led Mark to the living room. No one ever used the living room. The Archers didn't entertain. The room was tastefully decorated and the furniture was formal and appropriate for the mood of the restored townhouse. It seemed like the right place for solemn news. She beckoned with her hand for Mark to sit in a wing chair. She sat near him in a flowered love seat. "What do you know about Bob?" she asked.

"Mrs. Archer. It's not easy for me to say this. Your husband's body . . ."

Mark didn't get any further. Judy collapsed in on herself and sobbed uncontrollably. Mark didn't know what to do next. He didn't have much experience at this. No one in his family of origin had died. He was not an expert in counseling survivors so he did what came naturally. He sat quietly until she regained control. Judy got a hand towel from the kitchen and a glass of water and came back into the living room and returned to the love seat. Her face and eyes were red, but she was breathing normally and she fixed her gaze on Mark.

In her gaze were a hundred questions.

"How much do you want to hear?" Mark asked her with a newly found wisdom.

"Was he killed?"

"We think it was a suicide."

The floodgates reopened. Mark knew that this was going to be a long session. He relaxed in his chair and waited for Judy to settle down again.

"Would you like a cup of coffee or anything?" Judy asked.

"Yes, I would," Mark replied.

He followed her into the kitchen and sat at the small square kitchen table where Judy and Bob had eaten almost all of their meals together. It was an antique table with inlaid trim. Two chairs were placed in opposite positions. The coffee was already prepared. Judy poured coffee into two mugs and put sugar and non-dairy creamer on the table. "Anything else?" she asked.

"This is fine. Thank you," Mark answered. For the first time he noticed Judy Archer. He admired her poise in light of the circumstances. And he couldn't help but notice how pretty she was. "Should I go on?" he asked.

"I guess I need to hear it all, don't I?"

"There's not much to tell. I was hoping that you could fill in some of the details when you feel up to it. Two boys found your husband's body in the Des Plaines River on Saturday morning, but there was nothing in his pockets. We weren't able to identify him until early this morning. The best we can come up with is that he parked his car at the railroad station, walked along the tracks to a railroad bridge over the river, shot himself, and fell into the river."

"Bob shot himself?" Judy asked with a steady gaze.

"There was a bullet wound in the right temple. We found the gun. His prints were the only prints on it. Our coroner is pretty sure it was a suicide."

"Excuse me," Judy said as she left the kitchen. Mark heard her go upstairs. Soon she returned with a small box. "Bob kept a .22 in this box in the closet. He said that it was for my protection. He even made me go with him to a pistol range to load and fire it. It's not in the box."

The box was the original container for a Phoenix HP-22.

"I'm sure you'll have other questions, Mrs. Archer. I'll leave my card with you. Please call if you need more information. Ask for me, please. I'm sorry to put you through this now, but we'll need some directions regarding Dr. Archer's body and his car." Mark hated to use the word "body," but he couldn't think of a good substitute. "Have your funeral director call me. Is there anything that I can do for you now?"

Mark felt as though he was abandoning Mrs. Archer, but he knew she needed time to think things through. He left his card on the kitchen table, and stood to leave.

"Yes, there is one thing that you can do," she said as she approached him. "You can just hold me for a moment."

Mark was caught off guard. Judy was shaking. Her eyes were filling up again as she leaned her head on Mark's shoulder. He didn't know what to do next. He gently placed his arms around her and held her while she absorbed his strength. In a few minutes, she put her hands on Mark's chest and gently separated them. She escorted him to the front door and thanked him.

Kelly followed Judy to the bedroom where Judy collapsed on the bed.

Death wasn't a common topic in the Archer household. She always hoped that when the time came she would go first, but she hadn't even shared this.

Several hours later Mark called to tell Judy that no unexpected prints were found on the Taurus. Doc Spencer had formally declared the death a suicide, and Jeff Myers had decided not to pursue the matter any further.

Since Mueller's had the body, Judy decided to let them do the preparations. Bob would be cremated and his ashes interred at Rest Haven Cemetery in the city, not far from the Archer townhouse.

Judy was a Christian; Bob was not. He was raised in a Christian family that attended church regularly, but after junior high school Bob made excuses to stay home. Then he lost interest. In college apathy turned to defiance. His first course in philosophy convinced him that religion was just another point of view. Ever since they met this had been a sticking point for Bob and Judy. She got up early on Sunday mornings and went to church. On Wednesday evenings, she attended adult Bible class. Bob slept in on Sunday and resented waking up to an empty bed and eating breakfast alone. His resentment poured over to the church. The church was a competitor for Judy's time and they had precious little of that as it was.

Judy knew that Bob would reconstitute himself and come after her if she planned a Christian funeral. Besides, what could the Pastor say about his faith? She didn't even know whether the Pastor would conduct a funeral for an unbeliever who committed suicide. She heard stories about cemeteries that buried suicides in a remote part of the cemetery without headstones. Was there a special place in the Rest Haven Mausoleum for suicides? Should she schedule a burial service for Bob or just deliver his urn to Rest Haven? Perhaps her Pastor could help.

Scott Dressler was a second-career minister. He entered the seminary the same year that he retired from the Army. At forty-two, he felt that he still had plenty of good years to give to a second career, besides the Lord had called him in a very convincing way to prepare for the ministry. Pastor Dressler had phoned or visited Judy every day since hearing that Bob was missing. He was a great comfort to her. With good listening skills, he had answered her questions without sermonizing. She called the church office and made an appointment to come by in one hour.

The Pastor met her at the door to his office. It was a comfortable office. The walls were lined with shelves of books about theology. Two chairs had been arranged in front of the Pastor's desk. A box of tissues and a business card holder sat on a small table between the chairs. The chairs looked like hand-me-downs from a business office. They didn't match the desk—another hand-me-down. An old gray file cabinet stood in the corner next to a prie-dieu which Judy had once erroneously called a kneeling bench. A previous-generation computer sat on a table in the corner of the office surrounded by disks and CD's. The desk was cluttered with office equipment, manila files, and coffee mugs. The smell of coffee permeated the room. A "Mister Coffee" machine was on top of the gray filing cabinet and a stained half-empty pot was hot. A floor fan stirred the papers in the office as it oscillated around the room at low speed, but the air felt good. Pastor Dressler pointed to a chair and Judy sat down. "Coffee?" he offered.

"No thanks," she replied. "I don't know what to do about a service for Bob," she confessed. "I need your advice."

"Of course," Dressler answered. "The choices are entirely yours, Judy. I will conduct a church funeral for your sake, if you wish; however, considering Bob's view of faith it might be better to do a chapel service at Rest Haven, then a brief committal service at the mausoleum. You realize, of course, that I will have to speak of the promises of faith in general terms."

"Yes, I understand exactly what you're saying, Pastor." Judy realized that she had put the Pastor in an awkward position. What could she expect a Christian pastor to say at the funeral of an unbeliever?"

They worked out a few details regarding time and music, and then Judy left, somewhat relieved that the old taboos about suicide were not going to be a problem.

• • •

The Pastor was talking with the Funeral Director when Judy arrived. No one else was there. The service didn't begin for another thirty minutes, so Judy went to the table in front of the chapel where pictures of Bob and some flower arrangements were on display. The urn was on a separate table under a ceiling light. Each picture had a special meaning for Judy, but she was determined not to lose control. She had cried herself dry at home. She said a silent prayer for strength.

Mark Garrison was the first visitor to arrive. Judy hadn't expected him. Why was he here? She had to admit she was glad that he had come. "I'm glad you're here," she blurted out without thinking. "Actually, I'm a little surprised. Do you always invest this much of yourself in your work?"

"Well, actually, it's not work that brought me here. I'm not on the clock."

"I'm not sure what to say," Judy admitted. "Please come and see the pictures of Bob." Judy took him by the arm and led him to the front of the chapel. Once again, she felt his strength and it was comforting. She knew she could get through the hour.

"Is it painful to talk about Bob?" he asked.

"Not really," Judy lied. "He was a quiet man who was totally committed to his work as a scientist. He also had a passion for country music."

"What kind of scientist?"

"His field was genetics. The lab he worked for was contracted to the Human Genome Project. He didn't talk much about his work, especially in the past few years. Actually, his work was his mistress. I was falling behind. It was a problem for us."

"He must have loved his work." Mark immediately regretted the remark, but it was out there and there was nothing he could do about it. He knew Judy caught the meaning of his comment. Her stare lasted a little too long. Mercifully, another visitor took Judy's hand and they headed for the picture table.

"Judy, I don't know what to say." Bev Hudson had been Bob's lab partner for three years. Judy had been uncomfortable about Bob spending so much time with someone as attractive as Bev in such close quarters. She had entertained the thought that there might have been something between Bob and Bev, but now it didn't matter, so she wrote it off to an overactive imagination.

"There's not much to say, Bev, except 'Why?'"

"I've asked myself the same question over and over," Bev said, holding on to Judy's hand. Bev was a brilliant scientist who had earned her Ph.D. in genetics and had graduated from the same university as Bob. As a matter of fact, Bob had learned of her from a former professor and hired her when she graduated. She was twenty-eight and unique. Judy had never seen her in a dress. Even now, at Bob's funeral, she was wearing slacks and a blouse. Her short hair and tan skin gave her an athletic look, but Judy knew that she was a lab rat like Bob. She wore no make up, ate no meat, had no chemical habits, and didn't own a TV. Bob told Judy that Bev had a family secret that she only discussed with him, and then rarely. She never spoke of her family outside the lab and avoided all questions about the subject. Photography was her hobby. She occasionally went to the movies for entertainment. At 5'6" and 118 lbs. Bev was attractive. She lived in an apartment above a grocery story in walking distance from the lab. Bob didn't think that she had ever owned a car. She attended Mass regularly and was active in pro-life activities. Bev was unmarried and had no boyfriends. "It's at times like this that our faith is helpful." Bev eased into the subject, not knowing whether it was fair game for conversation considering Bob's viewpoint.

"I don't know what I'd do without it," Judy responded. "Do I take it that you're a Christian?"

"Yes, an active Christian. You?"

"Same."

"I don't want to keep you from the other visitors, Judy, but maybe we could have lunch together soon."

"I'll call you when the dust settles," Judy said, suddenly thinking that that wasn't a very good expression at a funeral.

I Walk in the Garden started to come out of the ceiling speakers and people headed for chairs. Pastor Dressler was true to his word. The chapel service was about ten minutes long. Bob's name was mentioned several times, in the opening remarks and at the closing. In between the Pastor pointed out the importance of being ready for the unexpected. When the ceiling music ended, the whole group proceeded to the Mausoleum. Pastor Dressler said a few more words quoting the "dust to dust" passage and the Funeral Director ceremoniously placed the urn in the cabinet. Everyone went their separate way and Judy was left to wrap up the final details with the Funeral Director. On the way to her car she decided that she wouldn't go to the townhouse for awhile. Mark Garrison's car was blocked between Judy's and another car. He was waiting patiently for her to pull away.

"Sorry, Sergeant Garrison, hope you haven't been waiting long," Judy yelled as Mark rolled down his window.

"Just a few minutes. Would you like to get a cup of coffee?"

It was just the excuse Judy was looking for to avoid going back to the townhouse. "Yes."

Mark followed Judy out of the cemetery, then pulled up alongside her car and motioned for her to follow him. He led her to a Dunkin' Donuts two blocks from Judy's townhouse.

"Hard to go home?" Mark asked.

"Yes. I dread what's coming—dealing with Bob's things and then the legal matters. And I can't make sense out of it. I just didn't see it coming. They say suicides are predictable, but either I was blind or Bob's death was impulsive. He didn't seem depressed. He didn't give his things away. He never talked about suicide."

"Were there any changes in his life recently? I mean, in his daily schedule?"

"Only his obsession with work. There were some days when he slept at the lab rather than come home. He rarely talked about his work so I don't know what the attraction was. I thought for a while it was Bev Hudson, but after today I'm convinced I was wrong about her. For the past several years Bob was distracted at home. He hasn't played his guitar in months and several country western concerts came and went without Bob even knowing it. We would have been going for marriage counseling if his inattention had continued."

"Maybe you should talk to Bev Hudson. As his lab partner, she may know what was going on. Is it possible that he was afraid of losing his job? Maybe he was overworking to keep his job."

"Not a chance. Bob was in great demand when he was hired at the lab. He had a reputation for his work in genetics. He just recently received a company bonus and was offered a position in supervision, but turned it down. The laboratory was his love."

"Why did the minister skirt the issue of Bob's faith at the funeral?"

"Bob was a skeptic about the Bible. He had long ago given up his affiliation with the church. Science and knowledge were his gods. He scoffed at the Biblical story of creation and the fall into sin and the promise of heaven. Whenever Biblical topics came up we ended in a heated argument. His disinterest was turning to downright disdain. Pastor Dressler knew about Bob's lack of faith and did the funeral as a favor for me. I thought he did a good job under the circumstances."

"Judy, I have to get back to the station. My work on your husband's case is complete now, but I wonder if I could call you again?"

"I'd like that."

"I'd like to think that you'd call me if you need another donut."

"It's a promise." Mark placed his hand briefly on hers and she responded by clasping his hand. They left the donut shop and went their separate ways. He couldn't help noticing that Judy looked back at his car as she drove out of the parking lot. He wondered if she was feeling what he was feeling.

5
Bio-Gen

It took only a day for Judy to recover enough to return to her job at the high school. Sorting through Bob's things could wait until school was out for summer vacation. Insurance, wills, and the rest would take their natural course.

The red light on her answering machine greeted Judy as she returned from her first day back to school. After taking Kelly outside on his leash, she came in and shed her school clothes then punched the play button. "Hi, Judy, this is Bev Hudson. Just wanted to see if you would like to get together. Call me at the lab, please."

Whatever it was that pushed Bob over the edge had to be related to his work, Judy mused. Perhaps Bev Hudson could help Judy get to the source of Bob's despair. Bev agreed to meet her on Saturday morning.

Judy heard Bev's knock before Kelly. That was unusual. Like most Welsh Corgi's, Kelly's hearing was acute, but Kelly was getting up in years. She went downstairs and opened the door. Bev was in jeans and a sweatshirt. "Hi. Come in. I'm glad you came." Judy led her into the kitchen where she had put out a coffeecake. "How do you take your coffee, Bev?"

"Black. Thanks. Is it stupid to ask how you're doing?"

"No, not at all. I appreciate it—really. I'm doing okay, I guess. Still trying to sort out why Bob did this. I've come to the conclusion that it must have been something at the lab. Any ideas?" Bev's response to Judy's question convinced Judy that there was nothing between Bev and Bob. There was no indication of shame or guilt. Judy was glad. In fact, Judy was beginning to think that they could become friends.

"Bob and I were working on different segments of the human genome. We rarely discussed our work. I know that recently Bob became more intense about his work and less communicative in general. Our supervisor has asked me to assemble Bob's notes and assemble his research papers for a general review by the supervisory staff and lab manager. I'm supposed to have it done by the end of this coming week. If I find anything that would shed light on Bob's state of mind, I'll let you know."

34

The letters W. W. J. D. were printed on the front of Bev's sweatshirt. Judy asked the meaning of the letters. "They stand for the question, 'What would Jesus do?'" This led them into a conversation about their respective churches. Bev was a committed Christian and active in Bible study. They agreed to meet again after Bev finished arranging Bob's records.

Bev couldn't imagine anything at the lab that would have caused Bob to kill himself. As far as she knew, his work was acceptable to his supervisor. They didn't discuss their respective research unless they needed to consult, which wasn't often. Bob had been more intense about his work over the past several years, but Bev didn't place much importance on that. What did Judy mean when she said it must have been something at the lab that caused him to do what he did? Perhaps she was denying a problem at home. Bev knew that Bob and Judy had some conflict about having a family. They also had some faith issues, but these are things that couples work out. They don't kill themselves over them. Maybe there was something else going on at home that Judy didn't want to admit.

The usual crowd was in the pool when Bev arrived. She got into her tank suit, took the mandatory cold shower, then walked down the stairs to the pool. The Master's group had already started their practice swim. Bev had been a Master's swimmer since college. She competed in some of the local meets, but didn't go to the meets out of town, much to the dismay of her coach. She was a good swimmer. After her session, she dressed, left the old Y building and walked to the lab.

Bio-Gen Research Laboratory was a small company as research labs go. They occupied the second floor of the Burrey Building, a modern commercial building surrounded by a well-manicured lawn. There was no security check at the main door, but the second floor was secure. The elevator and stairway on the second floor exited into a small hallway. At the end of the hallway was a glass door. On the side of the glass door was a card slot. Employees slid their ID cards into the slot and the door buzzed open. Visitors could press the visitor button and the receptionist who sat in plain view on the other side of the door buzzed them in. Once inside, another door led from the waiting lounge into the lab. The receptionist could lock this inner door with a switch at her desk, if necessary. It had never been necessary. Bev smiled at the receptionist and entered the lab. The room that Bob and Bev shared was one of three small lab complexes. Each consisted of a lab and two offices connected to the lab. The offices were identical in layout. Cabinets for storing s and files stood behind the door on one side. A small hanging closet opened behind the door on the other side. There was a desk-high file cabinet next to a small desk. Across from the desk was a computer table with state-of-the-art computer equipment. A swivel chair was trapped between the desk and the table so the employee could move from one to the other without getting up. The only distinction between Bob and Bev's offices was a recliner squeezed into Bob's office and a small refrigerator in Bev's office.

Bev opened her refrigerator and removed a container of yogurt and a can of V8, which was her usual breakfast. Sorting through Bob's things and assembling his research papers would take several days. It wasn't a task that she relished. Judy's remark stuck in her mind. Would she uncover something that would help them see into the mind of Bob Archer?

Clothing from Bob's closet went into a sealed hamper. A sport shirt and pair of cotton slacks were carefully folded and placed on his desk. The loafers Bob wore when he worked in the lab were put on the floor by the desk. From the shelf of the hanging closet Bev retrieved some toiletry items. There was nothing out of the ordinary in the hanging closet, she thought. Clothing and toiletries went into a box that was then marked for Judy's attention. Bob was a neatnic. His paper files were in perfect order. Each file was properly labeled and in the right sequence according to project and date. SOP files, vendor files, meeting notes; articles from journals; and others—all the files were where they should have been. She envied Bob his orderly mind. Part of her assignment was to make a written inventory of the files.

All scientists at Bio-Gen used the same computer equipment. 100MB Zip disks were filed in shallow drawers in cabinets according to date. All data was saved on Zip disks, and backed up on a network system. The computer staff did backups and virus updates daily. It wasn't Bev's assignment to read the data on Bob's disks, just to assemble and organize them so that the supervisors and manager could audit his work. Project numbers and dates were entered on the Zip disk labels. Bob had been working on project 314 for three years, so that number appeared on all the Zip disks in his cabinet. Dates were entered below the project number. As Bev recorded the individual dates on her inventory, she noticed that some dates were missing. She rechecked the Zip disk labels a second time covering the entire three-year period of his project. The missing disks covered a fourteen-month period. This wasn't like Bob. There had to be a logical explanation. A recheck of his desk, closet, and file cabinet did not uncover the missing disks.

Bev walked to the computer room. A single employee managed the entire backup system of Bio-Gen. She slid her card into the ID slot and was buzzed in. "Cary, can you check some data entry dates for me, please?" she asked the young man.

"What are you looking for?"

"I'm not sure. I just want to know if you have backup data for a fourteen-month period on project 314."

"You know that you can only review your own data," Cary told Bev in a polite tone of voice.

"I don't want to review the data, Cary. I just want to verify its existence." She handed him a sheet of paper with the dates in question.

"It'll take me a minute."

Bev sat down at the chair next to Cary's desk and watched him perform his magic. It wasn't a minute before he looked up with a puzzled expression. "I don't have any data for these dates."

"Can backup data be removed?"

"Yes, it can be deleted from remote stations, but only by the employee who entered the data originally. It's never been done before as far as I know. And it can't ever be removed from the archives."

"The archives?" Bev asked.

"The backup data that I manage is a working system—tied in through a network to each of the labs here. There is another backup system at the Bio-Gen main office that is an archive system. It stores all data permanently. It is a security thing. Backups in two locations in case of an emergency."

"Is there any way to know whether there is data for these dates in the archive system?"

"It will take me a while to check," Cary replied.

"Let me know, please."

It didn't long before Cary called Bev. No Project 314 files had been backed up for the fourteen months in question. Bev looked everywhere in Bob's office and the laboratory for some record of Bob's work during the fourteen months before his death, but she could find nothing. She decided not to report the missing research files to Bob's supervisor until the next day. She would hope to have an answer before then. She knew that Judy would be home after 4:00 p.m.

Bev walked to her apartment after work and got her mountain bike. The ride would clear her head. She couldn't get the missing files out of her mind. It took twenty minutes to ride to the Archer's townhouse. Judy wasn't home. Bev sat on the steps leading up to the front door of the townhouse.

"Hi, Bev. What a nice surprise," Judy yelled as she got out of her Escort. Bev took two armloads of groceries and Judy carried her school papers and negotiated the door and security code. Kelly was already at the door. Bev slipped her bike into the foyer as Kelly watched it warily. "Give me just a second, Bev. I want to change clothes. Raid the fridge, if you like."

Bev checked the refrigerator and found Gatorade. She poured a small glass and sat down at the kitchen table.

"It's a surprise to see you so soon, but I'm glad you came by."

"I wish it were just a social call, Judy, but I need a favor."

"Sure. What is it?"

"I've spent the day organizing Bob's things at the office. There's a box with some clothes and toiletries for you to pick up when you're over that way. And you'll need to make arrangements to have his recliner moved here, but that's not why I'm here. Something has come up that I don't understand. Bob's data files for the past fourteen months are not in his office. To make matters worse, there is nothing in the lab backup files to account for his work. The computer tech checked the main archive files and there is nothing there, either. I know that you have a computer here. I wondered if, by any chance, Bob was doing some work at home."

Judy used the home computer. Bob never touched it. "No, Bob didn't do any work at home. He told me once that wasn't allowed."

"The rules about that are pretty tight," Bev agreed. "The problem is that a lot of rules seem to have been broken here. Lab protocol requires that all research be recorded on disk every day. Bio-Gen backs up all the lab computers automatically during the night, and I have learned that all backup data is transmitted to a main archive at the home office during the night. In other words, there should be three sets of every day's work. No work for Project 314 has been recorded for the past fourteen months. I was hoping that the Zip disks might be here. Could you look around tonight and see if Bob brought any Zip disks home?"

"Sure. But there's something I don't understand. Doesn't anyone look over your shoulder? How do they know that you are working at all if fourteen months of research can be missing?"

"Actually, they don't. We have project meetings each month, but no one checks to see whether there is data in the backup system to support the project reports. It can happen, obviously."

Judy promised to search the townhouse for the files, but she knew that she wouldn't find anything. Bob had never brought anything home from the lab. And Judy had thoroughly cleaned the townhouse before the funeral.

6
The Disks

Mark didn't recognize the voice on the other end of the phone. "This is Officer Gallagher of the Wheeling Police Department. We have something out here that I think you should look at. It has to do with the man you pulled out of the Des Plaines River. Could you come out?"

"I'll be there in about an hour and a half," Mark replied. He hadn't thought about Dr. Archer for several days. Gallagher's call brought the whole matter back to mind. What could they have in Wheeling that would connect to the Archer case? Mark signed out on the ledger at Sue's desk and headed for Wheeling.

"I'm looking for Office Gallagher," he announced at the reception counter as he slid his card across the counter.

Without a word the officer lifted his phone and pushed a button. "Gallagher, you've got a Sergeant Garrison asking for you." He hung up the phone and pointed to a door at the end of the reception counter. The door buzzed as Mark approached it. Gallagher was standing on the other side of the door with his hand extended. He led Mark to a small interrogation room.

"Sergeant Garrison . . ."

"Mark, please."

"Mark, a boy came by here this morning with a file case that I think you should see. It's full of computer disks. Each disk has the name Archer and the number 314 on it. We know that you fished a Dr. Archer out of the river, so we think you ought to look at this."

Mark received the box from Gallagher. It was still coated with river scum. "Where did the boy find these?" Mark asked.

"He and his sister were water skiing behind their father's boat. The boy went down in a shallow section of the river. He saw the reflection of the sun on the file box and pulled it out near the bank. His father drove him by the station to drop it off. We didn't detain him, but we have his address and phone number if you want to follow it up."

Mark signed a release form and took the box and the disks back to Riverside. Had Jeff closed the case too soon? Was Archer's death more than a suicide? What was on these disks that Dr. Archer didn't want anyone to see?"

Jeff and Corky were out of the office. Mark decided to call Judy.

Judy had eaten alone since the funeral. She was pleased when Bev agreed to stay for dinner. Both women were adequate cooks, but on this night food took a back seat to conversation. Bob was the subject. While Judy was making stir-fry, Bev sat at the kitchen table and sorted through photographs. Although she was a brilliant scientist doing state-of-the-art research, she had her shoes off and her legs stretched out on the chair next to her. She looked like a teenager reading Seventeen. "Bev," Judy asked, "was there anything in Bob's behavior that suggested he wanted to die?"

"Nothing. I was thinking about that on my ride over here. They say that people leave hints before they kill themselves—sorry, Judy." It came out before she could stop it.

"I know. I have tried a million times to think of things Bob said, but he left no clues."

"Well, Bob did change," Bev said. "He was far more intense at work. And he made more field trips than usual during the past year. We were just talking about that at the last budget meeting."

"I wasn't aware of any field trips. They must have been day trips."

"No, overnighters."

"I know that he slept at the lab a number of times, but I didn't know that he was traveling."

Bev thought that it was best if she dropped the subject. In fact, Bev didn't know much about the trips, either.

The ringing of the phone broke the awkward silence. "Hello," Judy greeted.

"Hi, Judy. It's Mark Garrison. I have something that I'd like to show you. Would it be convenient to come by your place?"

"When, tonight?"

"Yes, if it's okay."

"I have company for dinner, Mark, but if you think it's urgent."

"I'm not sure. It can probably wait until tomorrow."

"Now you've got my curiosity up. If you hurry, you'll be in time for stir-fry."

Mark closed up his office for the night, took the box of disks, and headed for Judy Archer's.

"That was Sergeant Garrison. He's the policeman that was in charge of

Bob's case. He's coming over with something to show me. I can't imagine what it is. He sounded as though it could be significant. I hope you don't mind that I asked him to join us."

"If the stir-fry is soggy, it's your fault," Judy said as Mark stepped into the foyer. Kelly recognized Mark at once and strolled back to his rug in the kitchen. Judy led Mark into the kitchen and motioned toward the chair in the corner. Mark pulled up the chair then laid the file box on the table. Immediately Bev saw the label on the box: Archer-314.

"Where in all the world did you get that?" she asked.

"Some kids found it in the Des Plaines River. Somehow it found its way to Wheeling. Apparently Dr. Archer must have thrown it into the river thinking that it would sink. Instead, it floated all the way to Wheeling then got lodged in some branches. A water-skier found it and turned it in to the police. I picked it up there this afternoon."

"I'll bet they're Bob's missing files," Bev said with subdued excitement. "May I see them?" Mark slid the file box across the table. Before Bev opened the file box, she asked, "Is this evidence?"

"Of what?" Mark asked.

"I mean. Does this change the finding of suicide?"

"No," said Mark. "But it may help us understand Dr. Archer's reason for killing himself." He didn't want to stay on this line of conversation for Judy's sake. "Suppose we finish this conversation after dinner?" Actually, Mark was hungry. He hadn't had a home-cooked meal for awhile and the stir-fry smelled great.

After dinner Bev offered to clean the kitchen while Mark and Judy sat at the kitchen table with the file box of Zip disks. "Have you ever seen these before, Judy?" Mark asked.

"No," she replied.

"And you, Bev?"

"Yes. It's the box that Bob used at the office to store his working disks. The disks should all be labeled with the project number, date range, and Bob's name." They were.

"Is the data scientific mumbo-jumbo?" Mark asked.

"Not for me," Bev offered. "But it might be for you two."

"Could you decipher it?"

"Yes, but it covers fourteen months of research. It would take a long time.

I'd need approval from my supervisor to do it."

"Would you be willing?" Judy asked.

"Of course. I'll let you know what I can do."

Mark agreed to drop the file box off at the lab the following day.

Corky was already out, but Jeff was in his office when Mark came into the station with the filebox under his arm. He dropped a bag of Dunkin' Donuts on Sue's desk. "Jeff, have you talked to anyone from Wheeling?"

"Why would I talk to someone from Wheeling?" he asked.

"This filebox of computer disks was found in the Des Plaines River by some water-skiers and turned in to the Wheeling Police. I picked them up yesterday afternoon and passed them by Judy Archer and Dr. Archer's co-worker, a lady named Bev Hudson. They belonged to Dr. Archer. Apparently he tossed them into the river and they floated all the way to Wheeling."

"Some Odyssey," replied Jeff. "What are you thinking, Mark? Does this change our thinking about Archer?"

"I don't think so. It may give us some answers, though, about him. I'd like to let Dr. Hudson take a look at them. She can interpret the scientific jargon. Any problems?"

"Go for it. I don't intend to commit any more time or money to the Archer case. Anything from here on, Mark, is on your own time, okay?"

Bev's project was not at a breaking point. To take time away from her project would certainly put her behind schedule. She had two weeks of vacation coming to her, however, and had no specific plans. Reading fourteen months of research data was not her idea of a vacation, but her curiosity was killing her. If she could upgrade her old computer at home and do the research there, she could at least make herself comfortable in the process. She decided to ask her supervisor for a one week vacation. She would take her computer to the geek-genius who had rescued her before and get the RAM and processor upgraded. Her hard drive was okay.

Mark took the file-box to the Bio-Gen Lab. He rang the visitor's bell and asked for Bev. She escorted him to the conference room on the second floor. "Bev, I talked to the captain this morning. He is okay with releasing the disks to you. One thing—the case regarding Dr. Archer is closed. Whatever you discover on these disks will have no bearing on the coroner's ruling or the captain's decision to close the case, okay?"

"So why am I doing this, other than to satisfy my curiosity about Bob's death?"

"That's reason enough, isn't it? I'm also curious. Will you keep me wired in?"

"I suppose it is, and yes, I will. I will be doing this on my own. I've taken a one week vacation starting as soon as I can get my home computer upgraded—probably in a couple of days. If you're interested, I'll give you my address and number. You can keep in touch if you like."

"I'd like," said Mark as he handed his cassette recorder to Bev. She dictated her address and number, handed it back and got up to escort Mark to the front door. "One more thing, Bev. Can you tell me in a couple of sentences what it was that Dr. Archer did?"

Bev laughed. "No, not in a couple of sentences, but here's an overview. Bio-Gen is one of many labs subcontracted to the NIH. to do research in the Human Genome Project."

"The Human Genome Project?"

"The Human Genome Project is a collaborative effort with laboratories and scientists around the world attempting to map the human genome."

"What is a human genome?"

"A genome is all the DNA in an organism including its genes. Certainly you know what DNA is. Don't you use DNA matches to link suspects and victims?"

"That's for the city guys. We're just a small-town police force. I know that DNA is like a body cell fingerprint and fairly unique to each individual, right?"

"Right. DNA is found as tightly coiled threads in the nucleus of every cell. The threads are composed of paired strands of base pairs. There are 3.2 billion base pairs in the human genome and 80,000-100,000 genes. Just imagine a twisted ladder, or two serpentine drive belts in a car engine held together by rungs. Genes are pieces of DNA which contain the functional and physical characteristics passed from parents to kids."

"I'm getting dizzy. What was Dr. Archer doing?"

"Bob and I and hundreds of other scientists are mapping the genes to discover what effect specific genes have on our health or behavior. We were working on different chromosomes, however, so I am not as familiar with Bob's research as I will be in the next week."

"Is your research busy work, or is there an objective?"

"There are all sorts of benefits from this research: environmental, health, behavior, etc. As we discover which gene does what, we will be able to diagnose or even anticipate consequences of genetic problems and, with gene therapy, correct the problem."

"What is gene therapy?"

"Replacement of bad genes with healthy genes."

"Are we headed toward a society of perfect people?"

"Not in our lifetime," said Bev as she took Mark by the hand and led him to the door. "You have to go now so I can get back to work. Hope I haven't totally confused you."

"I should have paid more attention in science class."

"We've come a long way, baby," Bev said smiling.

When Bev returned to her office the phone was flashing with two messages. Aaron from NetTech had her computer ready and her supervisor wanted to see her. She opted for Aaron.

"Your computer is ready to be picked up," he said. "I upped the RAM to 128 and upgraded to a Pentium processor. You can run AT&T with this thing. I also defragged and scanned the hard drive. You ought to do that occasionally."

"You're great, Aaron. Thanks. Any chance you could drop it off at my apartment this evening?"

"Be there about 6:15."

Aaron had bailed Bev out on several occasions. He was a classic nerd, but Bev was gaining a real appreciation for the place of Nerds in the world. She decided to walk to her supervisor's office.

George was standing outside his office when she approached. He was a good scientist who had worked his way up to supervisor. The Peter Principle didn't apply to George—he was one of those rare individuals who could be moved from a specialized position to management without exceeding his level of competence, and he was also a good company man.

"What's up?" Bev asked. "You left a message on my machine that you wanted to see me."

"Hi, Bev. I met with the management team this morning. There's a lot of concern about Bob Archer's disks. Project 314 is important to us. Because Bob didn't backup his work, the disks that you have are our only records. We're anxious to know whether they are readable and what is on them. I'd like you to set your own project to the side, Bev, and do two things: Backup the disks as soon as possible, and make a full report to the management team on Bob's progress with 314. After we have your report, we'll assign Project 314. Take whatever time you need, but understand that this is a priority. Forget the vacation. You'll be on the payroll."

"George, I'd like to do this at home where there are fewer interruptions. I've had my computer upgraded to handle the volume."

"It's against policy to take work home, Bev. You know that. In this case, I'll allow it, but make sure that the disks are secure, and get them backed-up pronto, okay?"

Aaron was right on time. He set up Bev's system and turned it on. She was amazed at the speed with which the computer went through its startup cycle. "How much, Aaron?"

Aaron handed her the invoice. It was always lower than Bev expected. That and Aaron were the reason she stayed with NetTech. She wrote a check and walked Aaron to the door. "Thanks, Aaron," she said. "By the way. What can I expect from disks that have been on a river cruise?"

"I'd put them in the dish washer," he said. She thought he was kidding. Over his shoulder he called, "Won't hurt them." He high-stepped to his car and left.

Carefully, Bev lined up the disks in her dishwasher, set the water temperature to lukewarm, filled the soap reservoir to one-half, crossed her fingers and turned the machine on the short cycle, imagining the worst. The image of data running down the drain and George handing her a pink slip was clear in her mind. It was safer to leave the room rather than listen to the dishwasher destroying fourteen months of work. She intercepted the machine before the hot dry cycle and set the disks on a dry towel. They would not be read until tomorrow when they were completely dry.

Bev got up early to read the disks. They seemed to be dry throughout. Then came the moment of truth—she slipped a disk into her Zip drive, opened the drive from her word processor, and selected the first disk. The yellow light on her Zip Drive began flashing, then, as if by magic, the screen came alive with text. It worked! Bless Aaron. She called George to report the good news and promised to stay in touch with him. Bev had no idea what was ahead for her.

There were twenty-two disks in the filebox. Each disk contained 100MB of data or text. It took an hour and a half to sort them out. Eighteen of the disks contained numbers and letters in formats that only Bob and Bev and their colleagues could understand. The rest was text—a narrative of Bob's project. All the disks were arranged in chronological sequence. Subordinate projects were on separate disks. Bev knew that George would be interested in the research data, and Judy would be interested in the text. She came down on Judy's side and decided to read the text first. Four disks of text would take a long time to read. She scrubbed the filebox inside and out, then arranged the eighteen data disks by date in the box, then stacked the four text disks next to her monitor and entered the first disk in the Zip Drive.

Bev was uneasy. It came to her that she was about to look inside the soul of a very private man who had taken his own life because of something in these disks. She was sure that the text disks would give up the secret of Bob's suicide. Somehow she was on holy ground—a term that Bob would not have liked.

She decided to call Judy before she began her journey into Bob's recent past. Judy's machine answered so Bev left a message. Of course, Judy would be at school.

The first disk began with the label: Archer—Gene 314, Chromosome 17. As Bev pulled the daily entries into her word processor, it became clear that the disks were a kind of daily journal. Bob had methodically entered a narrative of his activities for the entire fourteen-month period. The entries were exhaustive. It was like Bob to be thorough. He didn't waste words. His grammar was concise. Nothing in the early weeks of Bob's work seemed out of the ordinary. Bob's research was a lot like hers: Study DNA samples with a particular interest in a certain gene segment. Although they were working on different chromosomes, the protocol was identical—acquire anonymous universal samples, determine properties, record results. Scientists all over the world were doing exactly the same thing. Eventually the entire genome would be mapped in this way.

The samples used in labs around the world came from the same six anonymous donors. The samples were cloned, studied, and reported. N.I.H. was the sponsor for Bio-Gen. Other agencies were sponsoring similar research. At some point, the results would be combined and the entire genome would be mapped. It was like a giant jigsaw puzzle with pieces farmed out to different people. Eventually, the segments would be combined and the picture would become clear.

Bob's work paralleled Bev's at the beginning. After the first day of full-time reading, Bev needed a break and a plan. If she were going to spend a week in front of the monitor she would need to exercise and plan her meals differently. Judy returned her call in the evening and they decided to walk each morning before Judy had to leave for school. Bev would forego Master's swim for a week, stock up on fruit and instant breakfast, and stay with the project for the duration.

• • •

Judy got to Bev's apartment at 6:30 a.m. wearing shorts, a tee shirt, and walking shoes. Bev had a sweatband across her forehead and was wearing a light running suit. She opted for modesty in her neighborhood. No sense inviting trouble. They had set thirty minutes as their limit. After some stretching exercises in the apartment, they began a brisk walk. Both women were in excellent condition and could talk easily while maintaining their pace.

"Nothing out of the ordinary," Bev replied to Judy's question about the disks. "I've read his reports from the first three months and he was making normal progress. As a matter of fact, my reports say about the same thing as Bob's. So far, I find nothing to indicate a problem. He's a good writer—to the point and easy to read."

"I wish I could say the same about his communication at home. We used to have long talks about important things, but lately he kept a lot to himself. I've been trying to relive the past fourteen months and some things are coming into focus. It's been about a year since Bob and I said or did anything of significance together. Whatever was going on began about a year ago. I don't remember any overnighters at the lab before then—or wherever they were. I should have been more alert to his preoccupation. I missed the signal."

"Me, too. It was the same at the lab. Bob and I ate lunch together for several years, but during the past year he often ate in his office. His trips away were predictable. He would make two trips at the end of each month, each for one night. He never discussed his business and it was inappropriate for us to discuss our projects unless we had technical consultations."

As they approached the grocery store below Bev's apartment, Bev invited Judy up for fruit. Judy declined and headed for her car. "Tomorrow?" Judy asked.

"Same time," said Bev. She went through the grocery store door instead of her apartment entrance and picked up some fruit for her next marathon computer session.

7
Mutation

The second day started like the first. Bob's research and activities were predictable, but at the beginning of the fifth month of his project something changed. He introduced new DNA samples. Bev couldn't believe what she was reading. All of the labs were studying the same anonymous donors. Unapproved samples were not part of the research study. There were no funds for piggyback research, yet Bob was studying DNA from other subjects. No reason was given in his report. He had sampled hundreds of donors and reported his activity without any explanation. Bev was glued to her monitor. She devoured each word as if she had just learned to read. Who were these people? Where had the samples come from? Why had Bob expanded his project? Who had authorized this? What was he looking for? There was something in his research that he hadn't reported. What was it?

Bev was uncomfortable and decided to go to the data disks to review the scientific entries for the first four months. The thought was tiring. Reading four months of scientific data would take a lot of time, but she was convinced that the answer to Bob's expansion was in the data. It became clear that Bob acquired the additional samples in the beginning of the fifth month, so the clue would be in the fourth month of his research.

Tired and ready for a break after four hours of reading scientific data, Bev peeled a banana and sliced an apple into quarters. To limber her stiff body, she did some stretching exercises, then sat down again on her ergonomically correct chair. She pulled the Zip disk out of the filebox and slid it into the Zip drive. In the fourth month Bob's research had shifted. In one of the approved samples, Bob had found a mutant gene, no. 15105, and he began reporting on the structure of the mutation. A base pair was missing in the DNA strand. Just what effect this mutation had on the donor Bob would need to determine.

Bev read until the day ended. She knew that she was mentally exhausted and still incredulous about Bob's project, but she needed to reserve her strength. There was much more data to read. She summarized her findings in her mind. Bob had discovered a mutation in Gene 15105 in one approved donor, then discovered that the same mutation occurred in all the approved donors. At some later time, Bob had secured hundreds of additional samples.

Things were getting interesting. Bev felt as though she was complicit in a prohibited project. Should she report her findings? Or should she finish reading Bob's narrative before she reported his work? She decided to continue reading the narrative before she said anything that would implicate Bob or embarrass Judy. So far, Bob had violated protocol in several ways. He was no longer studying the gene to which he had been assigned. He had expanded the sample base beyond the approved donors. And he had obviously erred. A mutation by definition was a structural change within a gene or chromosome not found in the parent. To have the same mutation in all approved donors would be an anomaly. Bob must have erred in his procedure. Perhaps she would find an explanation in the narrative. She'd switch back to the narrative tomorrow.

Bev had to force herself to keep pace with Judy. She was tired. She had slept on the edge, thinking about Bob's project. Judy was handling her grief very well and Bev didn't want to unload all of her concerns about Bob's project, but Judy was insistent about how things were going. "Bob's research took a bit of a side trip, I'm afraid."

"What kind of a side trip?" Judy asked.

"About a year ago he found a gene problem in his sample and expanded his study."

"Is this a problem?"

"Expanding the research could be. I don't know whether he had authority to do it. I'm still reviewing the disks. I wouldn't worry about it. He was a good scientist and I'm sure there is a logical explanation." Bev didn't believe what she was telling Judy. She would have known if it had been approved. It would have come up at a monthly meeting.

Judy seemed satisfied with Bev's answer. "Would you like to go to Bible study with me on Wednesday night? We're going to be starting a new study on Genesis. I would really like to have your company."

"I'd love to go, but give me a rain check. I'm afraid that reviewing Bob's disks is draining me mentally. I know that I wouldn't be up for a Bible study on Wednesday. How about in a week or two?"

"Great." Again, Judy took a pass on Bev's invitation for a fruit breakfast and headed for her car.

Having showered and dressed, Bev stationed herself in front of her computer. She wasn't as enthusiastic about the project as she had been the day before. Bob was venturing into dangerous territory. Perhaps there would be an explanation in his narrative.

Somehow Bob had secured DNA samples from Bio-Gen's Security Department for his analyses. All Bio-Gen employees were DNA typed for security purposes. The narrative gave no information about how Bob got the samples. Testing was highly confidential and the results were kept in the security department. Bev didn't want to think about the possibility that Bob had taken the samples without permission.

Every sample that Bob tested showed the same mutation in Gene 15105— a missing base pair in the DNA strand. There were no exceptions. Every sample was defective. Statistically, this was impossible. A common mutation was an oxymoron, and the implications of a common mutation were equally staggering. Gene mapping was being done in order to identify gene problems and correct them. How could a common mutation be corrected if there were no healthy 15105 genes? How could a comparison be made between a healthy donor and an effected donor if all donors were effected? What would be the basis of comparison? It would be impossible to determine the effects of a mutant 15105 unless somehow the base pair could be replaced or repaired and introduced into a human. Then the individual would have to be observed for physical or behavioral changes. Approval would be needed for human studies—all of which would take years.

Bev couldn't continue. She had to gasp for breath. The narrative was leading into murky waters. The analogy wasn't a good one. As a scientist, Bev knew clearly what alternatives Bob must have considered. To go the route of approval had several ramifications. First, Bob had already deviated from protocol and was subject to disciplinary action and possible dismissal. Second, approval would extend the project for years. Third, the implications of Bob's discovery were enormous. A mutant gene common to all samples, the effect or effects of which were immeasurable. Were the effects Physical? Behavioral? Beneficial? Harmful? Insignificant? What were the ethical implications of waiting to find out? On the other hand, what were the ethical implications of correcting the gene? Bev's head was swimming.

The pool was a place where Bev could clear her head. Master's swim was over, but the pool was open for community swim. Two lanes were roped off for lap swimming. There were other swimmers in the pool, so everyone had to do lap circles. It was frustrating for Bev, a Master's swimmer, to do circles. The whole circle swam at the speed of the slowest swimmer. Fortunately, everyone in Bev's circle was a good swimmer. Bob and his research were forgotten, at least for awhile. Maintaining her patience in the lanes and not swimming over the top of the older gentleman ahead of her became her first priority. Her muscular body glided through the water like a fish. The tank suit revealed her perfect shape. After swimming a mile and a half, Bev hoisted herself out of the pool and relaxed in the spa before showering. Having worked up an appetite, she stopped by the grocery store on her way back and picked up some fresh vegetables for a salad, which she ate in the living room, something she seldom did. She needed a break from the routine—and from Bob Archer.

It was after 2:00 p.m. when she felt like confronting the computer again. Her head was clear enough to make some decisions. She would tell no one but Judy about what was surfacing until the review of the disks was completely done. George would be calling and she would have to come up with some way to stall him, yet convince him that she was earning her salary.

Bev resumed her review of the narrative. For the next two months, Bob focused his energy on finding a way to repair or replace the missing base pair. This was Bob's forté. His background and experience had been in gene repair. He understood genetic codes and their chemistry. Bob knew that if he had reported this project out of his lab, there were few people at Bio-Gen who could have handled it. It was his project and he wanted to stay with it to the end.

It was apparent from Bob's narrative that he was investing himself too heavily into the project. Bev noticed that his writing was changing, his sentences were more staccato. Clarity was missing, almost as if to disguise his work. The narrative would have confused a layperson. Bev knew science, and Bev knew Bob. Something was changing in Bob. He was clearly frustrated by his lack of success in repairing the base pair. One experiment after another failed. Bob never experienced failure like this. How could she have missed this? How did Bob hide this from her and from Judy? If she had known that he was going through this, what would she have done or said to him? Certainly Bob knew that she would have been very uncomfortable working this far outside of lab protocol. He chose not to risk telling her. How much should she tell Judy?

Sleep came more easily. Her body was at the exhaustion point. The swim had also helped. She woke to Judy's knock at her door. Staggering to the door in her Teddy, she apologized for not being ready. "Come in, Judy. I just woke up. Sorry. Let me get some clothes on."

"Would you rather just have breakfast and talk?" Judy asked.

"Frankly, yes."

Judy went downstairs to the grocery store and bought some bagels while Bev splashed water on her face and pulled on some jeans and a sleeveless pullover. She came into the kitchen barefooted and curled into a chair while Judy cut the bagels and sliced some melon.

"I need to talk to someone, Judy, but what I have to say may not be what you want to hear."

Judy sat down in the chair opposite Bev and looked at her curiously.

"Yesterday I said that Bob had stretched the limits. You should probably know that he went over the edge where convention is concerned." Bev told Judy everything that a layperson could understand in as tactful a way as possible. What she didn't tell Judy was that Bob had accessed the employee's DNA samples. The repair research was not funded by Bio-Gen, so he was working under false pretences.

"Was he in deep enough to get into trouble with the law?" Judy asked.

Bev hoped that Judy wouldn't go there, but there it was. "Possibly."

"What could that mean now?" Judy asked.

"Nothing for Bob, of course, but it could shut down Bio-Gen, and destroy Bob's reputation," Bev answered.

"A lot of people would get hurt, wouldn't they?"

"Yes, me included."

"Who knows about this besides us?"

"No one, but I'm out on a limb. My supervisor expects me to make a duplicate set of Bob's disks for Bio-Gen. And he wants regular reports from me. So far, he's gotten zip and I haven't copied the disks. I'm hoping to get the whole story before I have to make a report."

"Bev, you're a good friend, but there is no sense in going out on a limb. You've got your career to protect."

"I've thought about that day and night. Frankly, what Bob discovered is major. It needs to be known. What concerns me is what I haven't read. There's nothing here to kill yourself for. I want to know where it leads. I'm going to stay with it for as long as I can. George is a scientist. He'll understand."

Judy felt helpless. She didn't know what to do or what to say. Bev was becoming a good friend. Judy walked around to Bev's side of the table and massaged her neck, then went home. For some reason, Judy felt like calling Mark Garrison. When she had learned about Bob's death, he had been her strength. She slipped out of her clothes and went upstairs and lay down on the bed. Kelly didn't attempt the stairs. He lay at the bottom and watched Judy's door. With the portable phone she called the Riverside Police Station. Mark was not there. She fell asleep.

The phone woke her from a deep sleep. It took a moment before she realized why Mark was on the other end. "Oh, Mark, I'm sorry, I was in a deep sleep. Thanks for calling."

"Sorry I woke you, but you called me."

"You said that you wanted to stay wired in on Bob's situation, so I thought I'd give you an update."

"The phone's not the place. Could we meet somewhere?"

"Where do you suggest?"

"There's a wooden walkway that surrounds the pond at Riverside Park. I like to walk on it. Can you get away from school at lunchtime and join me tomorrow?"

"Not easily, but I'll be there."

"Good. See you then."

The pond was spring fed. The walkway had been added when a prominent citizen left money for the project. It was a good idea when it was done, but apparently no money had been left for maintenance. The railings were wobbly, and some of the boards sagged under heavy weight. Youngsters were catching sunfish off the walkway, and sweethearts were walking arm in arm. Frogs, turtles, and other water life were splashing around and some turtles were sunning on logs. In sight of the pond was the City Hall. Secretaries and clerks lunched on picnic tables on one side of the pond, while others walked their lunches off. Mark was sitting on a picnic bench when Judy parked her Escort and walked toward him. "Hi," she greeted. He stood up and took her hand.

"Hi, yourself. Have time for a walk?"

She let him take her by the hand and lead her to the walkway. Once on the walkway, it was no longer necessary to have help. She thought about loosening her grip on his hand, but didn't. Neither did Mark. Without a word, they walked hand in hand around the pond. Judy told Mark about Bob's work, but didn't elaborate on his infractions. Mark read between the lines. "It doesn't sound as though you're comfortable with what Bob was doing."

"Is this between us?" she asked as she released his hand and faced him.

"Of course, Judy."

She told him everything.

Bev had set aside two of the data disks when she arranged them in the filebox. All but two of the disks had the same information on the labels, except for the dates. Two of the disks, however, had additional numbers. One of the disks had the number P061738; the other disk had 323412115. The added numbers were handwritten on the labels just below Bob Archer's name, project number, and date. The dates on both disks were out of sequence with the rest of the data disks. In fact, they were open-ended. Bob had recorded a date followed by a hyphen suggesting that the project or projects recorded on these disks were in process. Her plan was to read these after she finished the narrative disks.

8
Harley

"More of the same?" he groused as the guard slid his breakfast tray onto the dumb waiter in his door.

"Be glad you're alive to eat it, Harley," the guard shot back.

The disposable recycled paper tray was sectioned for different foods. Breakfast consisted of sliced beef on toast in a cream sauce, peaches in juice, and black coffee in a paper cup. Nothing was hot. No second helpings. He got up from his bunk and used the commode. One of the few advantages on Death Row was a single cell. In a single cell there was room for a chair and a small table for the TV and radio. And no one else used the commode. You never knew what to expect with a roommate.

Harley was a nickname that he got when he bought his first motorcycle. It stuck with him. No one on the floor knew him by any other name. Officially, he was a number. He couldn't remember when he wasn't a number. First, in the Army, then in one prison after another. He would always be a number—for as long as always lasted. On Death Row always came sooner rather than later.

The guard returned in an hour for the tray. Once all eating utensils were accounted for the guard dumped the refuse in a can pulled by an orderly behind him. "You've got a visitor, Harley. Get dressed. I'll be back to get you in fifteen minutes. Be ready."

Death Row inmates didn't get many visitors. Most families erased their names from the family Bible. Harley didn't care. Visitors were a pain. It meant putting on prison orange, being shackled and then led to a "secure" room in the Death Row visiting section. Visitors sat on the other side of a glass pane and conversations were held over the telephone for fifteen minutes—no longer. Walking, sitting, and talking on a phone were awkward with ankle chains and handcuffs. Only visitors approved in advance by the prisoner were authorized. They had too many enemies.

Harley vaguely remembered the man on the other side of the glass. He was wearing a clergy collar. Harley turned at the door to leave when he saw the collar, but the guard pushed him into a chair. The look in Harley's eyes was as cold as steel. He fixed his gaze on the man without saying anything. His face was expressionless. The pastor picked up the phone and held it to his head. Harley didn't. The pastor motioned to Harley to pick up the phone. Harley raised his middle finger, then picked up the phone. "What in the hell do you want?" he growled.

"You don't remember me, do you, Harley?"

"Why should I remember you?"

"I'm Rev. Dressler. You asked for a minister to come to visit you. I have been to see you several times, Harley."

"For what?"

"Do you remember me, Harley?" Harley ignored his question. Something was very wrong. Harley was acting as though they had never met. Dressler had been to see him every month for almost a year.

"I remember your face. That's about it. What do you want?"

"Is there anything that you want to say to me, Harley?"

"Yeah, get lost." Harley banged on the door for the guard. When the door opened he got to his feet and returned to his cell.

Dressler decided that he would return if Harley wanted to see him again, but that he would not schedule another monthly visit. He didn't know what to make of the change that had come over Harley.

When Harley got back to his cell, he lay down on his bunk and tried to remember why the minister looked familiar. It didn't come back to him. He threw his oranges over his chair. On the back, in black stenciled letters was his number: P061738.

Bev was getting frustrated with the narrative. One experiment after another had failed for Bob. His quest for a repair of cell 15105 was going nowhere. Bev felt his pain. She decided to leave the narrative for awhile and look at the two data disks with the strange numbers starting with the disk bearing the number P061738. It wasn't long before she wished she hadn't.

The beginning of the disk both shocked and delighted Bev. First, the disk was not data at all, but more narrative. Second, it was apparent that by the time Bob wrote this narrative he had found a repair for 15105. What shocked her was that he intended to use the "fix" on a human subject without any tests or approval. She noted his own words:

There is no way that I can set up an experimental protocol. I've gone too far with this. Whatever I do, my chances of maintaining access to a lab are gone once my work is known.

If the fix is successful, I will be able to turn over a complete project—discovery and repair of the mutation. Then, like it or not, they'll have to proceed with the project, even without me. I've got to find subjects with nothing to risk.

That was it. The number P061738 looked familiar to Bev. Not the number itself, but the format. It was the same kind of number assigned to her brother at Riverside Correctional Institute. He had a number that began with P0 followed by five digits. The number on the disk was the number of a prisoner, probably at Riverside. But, how did Bob get a prisoner at Riverside to cooperate with his project?

Bev hadn't seen her brother for almost three weeks. It was time for another visit. She needed to know how a visitor could gain access to an inmate.

For Bev going to Riverside was like going home. She had grown up in a small town and missed the slower pace. Her bus stopped at the Riverside train depot then made several more stops before it arrived at the Riverside Correctional Institute, a maximum security state prison. Citizens of Riverside had opposed the prison when it was built, but it proved to be good for the town. It quickly became one of the town's top employers. Visiting her brother had mixed blessings. She was the only visitor he had, as far as she knew, and she thought he liked it when she came. But visiting prison was intimidating. Except for one of the visiting room guards, the others were courteous. The one that Bev didn't like was sullen and uncooperative. He seemed to enjoy putting her and her brother in the most crowded section of the visitor's room, even when there were unused sections. She wanted some distance from other visitors on this trip. She needed to talk about P061738.

The bus pulled up to the sally port and Bev and two other women got off. The outer gate opened and the three women stepped inside. The outer gate closed and the inner gate opened. The women walked down a long sidewalk surrounded by a high chain-link fence topped with rolled razor wire. They entered the building and stepped into the visitor reception room. On the left were benches. Lockers lined the wall. On the right was the reception desk. Bev approached the desk and announced her purpose—to visit her brother. She gave his name and number. The officer behind the desk pulled his information up on the computer and verified her name on his visitor list. Without a word he slid a token across the desk. Bev knew the routine. She opened a locker and stored her fanny pack, watch, and necklace, then closed and locked the locker. Metal in her shoes set off the metal detector and so she had to remove her shoes and allow the clerk to pass them by the detector. The guard stamped the back of her right hand with an invisible mark, returned her shoes, then turned to the next visitor.

After putting on her shoes, she approached a metal door and waited. The door slid to the right admitting Bev into a passageway. It closed behind her. She held her right hand up to a black light. The guard on the other side of the window activated the door leading into the visitor's room, then closed it behind her. She walked down a short corridor to the guard's station and announced her brother's name and her locker key number. The sullen guard was not on duty. The guard was separating groups with several chairs between them. She assigned Bev to Row 2, chair 2. The room looked like a maze. Prisoners were separated from their guests by a meandering three-foot high wooden wall. Visits to men in the regular population were limited to one hour. Physical contact was allowed at the beginning and end of each visit, but nothing could pass between visitors and inmates. Guards were very strict about the rules. Bev waited fifteen minutes before her brother came through the screening door. He was searched and sent to a chair on the other side of the short wall between them. He waved when he saw her. Bev waved and stood up to hug her brother.

Bev's brother had been a troublemaker since he was born. He tested everyone and everything. This was not his first scrape with the law, but it was his first time in prison. He had already served three years and expected to be eligible for parole after two more years. He and two other men had beaten a store clerk while robbing his store. They were all drunk at the time and had been asked to produce identification to purchase beer. Instead, they beat up the clerk and stole beer. The clerk was permanently disabled from the beating. He was a star on his high school football team. The town was incensed.

"Hi, Sis," Bill Hudson greeted.

"Hi, Bill," Bev replied as she gave him a long hug. Bev was all the family Bill had. His parents refused to see him in prison and had stopped writing to him. He never spoke of them. As far as Bev knew she was his only visitor. The girl that he had been engaged to had married a mutual friend.

"You came a week early. I wasn't expecting you until the end of the month."

"Something came up at work that I need to talk to you about. Besides, I miss you. Are you okay?"

"I have a new cellmate. My old partner got kicked down to the floor." Bill was on the honor tier where the inmates had keys to their cells and could come and go as they pleased except during headcount. "The new guy is older and quieter. I think it's going to work out. What's this about your work?"

Bev explained the whole situation regarding Bob Archer, including the references to P061738. She asked how Bob Archer could get access to an inmate. Bill just stared at her quietly. Bev knew something was wrong. "What is it, Bill?"

"I didn't think it would be a problem."

"What do you mean?"

"Bob Archer wrote to me about a year ago. He had seen my number on one of my letters to you and said that he needed to talk to me. He asked me to put his name on my visitor's list. Next thing I knew he was out here. He told me that he was working on an important project that was very confidential. He said that I couldn't even discuss it with you. He needed a human volunteer, preferably someone on Death Row. Could I help him? All I would have to do is to get a Death Row inmate to agree to be a guinea pig and put Archer's name on his visitor's list."

"You got P061738 to agree to Bob's experiment?"

"Yes. His name is Harley. He's as bad as they get. They don't allow him out of his cell except for one hour of exercise each day—alone, under guard. The orderly who works Death Row was my former cellmate, Wayne Burroughs. He got a note to Harley. Harley thought it was a kick. Archer was seeing Harley once a month. I got out of the loop except for the envelopes."

"What envelopes?"

"Every month when Archer came to see me, he passed me a small envelope. Burroughs got it to Harley, and then Archer would visit Harley a week later. This went on for about ten months, then Archer stopped coming. I guess that's when he took a dive."

"You might have gotten caught."

"Stuff passes from visitors to inmates in this room. The guards are too busy to see it all."

"Do you know this Harley personally?"

"Just by reputation. My former cellmate says he's bad."

The guard reminded them that time was up. Bev stood up and hugged Bill for a long time. On her way back to the bus stop, she was in a daze.

The phone was ringing as Bev climbed the stairs to her apartment. It stopped before she could get to it and the caller hung up without leaving a message. The message light was flashing, however, and the number three appeared on the screen. Bev poured herself some Gatorade and ate a cereal bar. The minute she stepped into the apartment she remembered that she had not called Judy about her trip to the prison. No one had been here when Judy came for their morning walk. She picked up the phone and pushed the play button. The first call was from Judy. She'd call her back. The second call was a marketer with an important message. The third call was George. She would call him back. She opted for Judy, but there was no one home. Of course, she was at school. "I'm terribly sorry about this morning. I'll explain everything if you'll call me when you get home," Bev said to Judy's machine. She then called George.

"Bio-Gen. George speaking."

"George, this is Bev. You left a message on my phone." Bev knew why he had called, but didn't want to answer his questions.

"It's been awhile since I've heard from you. I was expecting to get a copy of Bob's disks and a report on your progress."

"I'm sorry, George. It's taking longer than I expected to get through the disks. So far, there is nothing extraordinary," Bev lied. It came suddenly. She had not decided whether to be complicit in Bob Archer's activity, but she was now committed. The implications were forming in the back of her mind as she talked to George and she was uncomfortable.

"I need those disks, Bev. I'm getting some pressure here about the missing data. When can you get them to me?"

"I won't keep you waiting, George." She hung up at the end of the sentence. She knew that wouldn't satisfy George and that he would be at her doorstep. She'd have to pick up the pace, then decide what course to take.

With reluctance, Bev went back to the disk with the number P061738. As the narrative unfolded, Bev became glued to the screen. She wanted to know more about her brother's involvement and the mysterious envelope transfers to Harley. After three hours, the phone rang. Bev was glad to be interrupted. She needed time to absorb what she had read.

"Bev, this is Judy. You're excused. I assume something came up."

"Judy, I am so sorry. I needed to make a trip to Riverside and in my rush to the bus I completely forgot about our walk. I've been a bit distracted lately. I need to see you."

"I have Bible study in about an hour. Would you like to go with me? We could get something to eat afterward."

"Yes."

"I'll pick you up in about forty-five minutes. Can you be ready?"

"I'll be ready. Thanks, and thanks for understanding about this morning."

"See you later."

Bev shut down her computer and the Zip disk popped out of the drive. She decided that she would make a full set of disks on the following day, but would not turn anything over to George. She would discuss everything with Judy and Mark Garrison before surrendering the disks. She called Staples and placed a phone order for two dozen Zip disks. They would deliver the disks tomorrow.

Judy was on time. The drive to the church didn't allow enough time for Bev to download on Judy. Anyway, she didn't want Judy distracted during the Bible study and decided to update her at dinner.

The church was typically small. Situated on a large well-groomed lot, the building was all brick. It had a dramatic inclining roofline and elevated cross. Bev didn't remember the name of the minister who officiated at the funeral for Bob until Judy drove past the church sign. It was Scott Dressler. He would be leading the Bible study on Genesis.

There were eleven in the class. Most were older than Judy and Bev. Bev was embarrassed to be without her Bible. She asked for a Bible and Pastor Dressler handed one to her. The study was more lecture than discussion which suited Bev just fine. Dressler was on the third chapter of Genesis. He began by quickly summarizing the previous lessons. God had created all things in six days, then rested on the seventh establishing the Sabbath. His first humans were created in his own image. The second chapter ended with God's warning not to eat from the tree of the knowledge of good and evil. Judy knew all this from Sunday school and confirmation studies and her mind wandered. She was not focused on the study. Handouts were passed around for the night's lesson on the fall into sin and its consequences. Pastor Dressler reminded the class that the basic nature of creation and mankind would be altered forever as a result of the fall. He fast-forwarded to chapter five and had a volunteer read verses one through three:

This is the written account of Adam's line. When God created man, he made him in the likeness of God. He created them male and female and blessed them. And when they were created, he called them "man." When Adam had lived 130 years, he had a son in his own likeness, in his own image; and he named him Seth. (NIV Genesis 5:1-3)

Bev's mind cleared long enough for her to hear verse three for the first time. What did it mean that God created man in his own image, but Adam had a son in his own image? She asked Pastor Dressler.

"The image of God was altered by the fall into sin," Dressler explained. "All children born after Adam and Eve were created in the image of their fallen parents. Thus all humanity has a fallen nature that can only be repaired by God."

The rest of the class was a blur for Bev. She could not get past the message of chapter three. Something happened to humanity at the Fall, which changed its basic nature, a nature that only God can repair.

"You seemed distracted this evening, Bev," Judy noted as they drove away from the church. "Would you like to stop at Denny's for dinner?"

"Anywhere where we can talk would be fine," Bev answered.

Denny's was about two blocks from the church. The high school age boy who greeted them led them to a booth by the front window and set menus on the table. "I like Pastor Dressler," Bev said.

"He's a sincere man. With Pastor Dressler what you see is what you get. His sermons are sometimes a little dry, but he makes up for it in sincerity. And he really cares about people. Speaking of Pastor Dressler ..." Judy nodded in the direction of the entrance to the restaurant. Scott Dressler was entering with another man. He caught Judy's eye about the same time that she saw him. He gave her a short wave and smile, then followed the host to a table within view of Judy.

"I have a lot to share with you, Judy. The information on the disks is getting more and more bizarre." Bev seemed very serious. Judy leaned forward to listen. She told her about Harley and her brother. Then she shared what she had learned from the disk with Harley's number.

"Bob set up a courier system at R.C.I. He needed volunteers with nothing to lose, so he enlisted my brother to make contact with a Death Row inmate. Then he arranged to get an envelope to the inmate, Harley, through my brother once a month. After that he visited Harley personally. The envelope contained an encapsulated liposome—a small capsule no larger than a pencil eraser which, when taken orally, could repair cell 15105. Apparently Bob had no trouble passing the small package to my brother during regular visits."

"I can't believe what I'm hearing. He never mentioned anything about R.C.I. I didn't know that he had ever been there."

"He couldn't tell you about this, Judy. He didn't tell anyone. He was already in way too deep. Human trials of an untested gene therapy are unheard of and very dangerous. We are dealing in the twilight zone with genetic therapy. That's why he needed subjects with nothing to lose. What amazes me is that he found someone willing to go along."

"What happened to Harley?"

"Bob saw him once a month, usually the week after he passed the envelope to my brother. He was looking for changes in Harley's health or behavior. He didn't know what effect the gene mutation had on human beings. All he knew was that every human sample he tested was missing a base pair at gene 15105. He had repaired the base pair and now needed to know what the result would be. All he knew about Harley was that he was a psychopathic killer and a bad apple. Apparently, Harley's health was excellent, except for some heart history. Harley was going through a series of mandatory appeals and didn't expect to be executed for several years, so Bob had time to observe him for changes in his health or personality. It didn't take long for Bob to see results."

"Did Harley change?"

"You wouldn't believe it, Judy. I haven't finished listening to the disk, but Bob reports significant changes in Harley's behavior, and improvement in his health."

Bev noticed that Pastor Dressler was standing at his table and shaking hands with the man who was with him. The other man left and Pastor Dressler approached their table. "Hi, ladies," he greeted. "Would I be interrupting a private conversation if I joined you?"

"Please, sit down," Judy said with little enthusiasm.

"I want to thank you for joining our Bible study tonight, Bev," he said sincerely. "I hope you'll return."

"It was interesting," Bev replied without making a future commitment.

"I really didn't come over to interrupt. It's late and I've been burning the candle at both ends. My family has forgotten what I look like. Too many classes, meetings, and visits to the prison." He got up to leave.

"I didn't know you made visits to the prison," Judy said in an inquiring way.

"I'm only visiting one inmate right now, but I go whenever a prisoner wants to see a Lutheran minister. I'm not sure I'll see this one again. He's on Death Row. He's had quite an experience there." Both Bev and Judy snapped to life. "His nickname is Harley—after the motorcycle, I suppose. A real conversion story, but you're not interested in that. Have a nice evening. See you in church, Judy." Again, he rose to go.

"Yes, it is interesting. We know so little about people like Harley. Tell us more, if you can," Judy asked, hoping that the pastor would continue.

Pastor Dressler sat down again and shared his observations of Harley over the period of his visits. "I was called by the prison chaplain to see Harley. Apparently, he had had some kind of religious insight and wanted to talk to a minister. I went out there and found a man who was utterly confused. The chaplain warned me that he was mean and obscene. I wasn't thrilled about seeing him, but when I got there he was as meek as a lamb. Through the glass I could see tears on his cheeks as he told me the horror of his life. He was truly apologetic for what he had done—the lives he had taken, some of which the authorities didn't even know about, and the people he had hurt. He poured it out. It was as if he had been waiting for a lifetime to purge himself of his heinous behavior. I heard his confession and gave him absolution on the first visit. In later visits, he became more and more eager to know about God and what God expects from him. Every time I came by he amazed me with his insights and concerns for others. He even told me that his health had improved. Until yesterday."

"What happened yesterday," Judy asked. Both women were gazing at Scott Dressler.

"Yesterday he made an obscene gesture, used profanity, and seemed uninterested in my visit. I don't even know whether he recognized me, or what caused the change. I don't plan to visit him again unless he requests it. Listen, I've bored you ladies long enough. I really must go." Scott shook their hands and left the restaurant.

"I can't believe it," said Bev. "Obviously, Pastor Dressler didn't know about Bob's trial, but his observations are parallel to Bob's. Once Harley began taking the fix, Bob reported that his behavior and physical health changed almost at once. The man who was the demon of Death Row became a model prisoner. I'm going to see if Bill's former cellmate noticed the same change."

"What do you make of it, Bev?"

"I'm too much of a scientist to make quick judgments, Judy, but apparently Bob found the change in Harley's behavior significant. I still have more to read on his disk." Bev hadn't planned to see her brother so soon after her last visit, but reports about Harley were compelling. She had one thing to do before she went to the prison, however. As soon as the delivery from Staples arrived, she would make copies of the disks.

When Judy arrived for their walk, Bev was eating a fruit breakfast. Judy got a small plate out of the wall cabinet and put two slices of cantaloupe on the plate. "Are you walking today?" she asked.

"You bet."

"Any ideas about Harley? I haven't been able to think of much else since Pastor Dressler's conversation last night."

"Me, too. Harley was taking the gene therapy that Bob provided. His behavior pattern changed. Bob also recorded a behavioral change. He didn't draw any conclusions from it, but I haven't finished that disk. I'm going to make a duplicate set of disks for safekeeping, Judy, then go out to R.C.I. and see my brother again. I want to hear from his former cellmate who saw Harley every day. Would you be willing to keep the duplicate disks at your house?"

"Sure, but why?"

"You know. They tell you never to keep backup disks with the originals. For security reasons."

After their walk, Judy got into her car as Bev approached the door leading up to her apartment. Her landlord stepped out of the grocery store and called to her, "Miss Hudson, there's a delivery for you in the store."

Bev picked up the box of disks, showered, and got dressed. It took about an hour and a half to copy all of the disks. She put the new set into a cardboard box, marked the box and taped it shut. She would give it to Judy in the morning. Then she checked the R.C.I. bus schedule. She could get a bus at 11:00 a.m.

"I didn't expect you back so quickly," Bill said as he hugged his sister. "What's up?"

"I'm still studying Bob Archer's disks, Bill, and there are some strange things happening. I need to talk to your former cellmate—the one who's an orderly on Death Row. Can you arrange to have him add my name to his visitor's list?"

"Not really. He's not here."

"Where is he?"

"He was paroled. I don't know where he is. He's got to be in the state, but I don't know where."

"Did he have a home somewhere?"

"He had a girlfriend in Bloomington who wrote to him. He might have gone there, if his parole officer let him."

"I've forgotten his name."

"Wayne Burroughs."

9
The Orderly

Bev made small talk with Bill for another twenty minutes, then hugged him goodbye. The Riverside bus was waiting at the sally port when she came out of the gate. She got off at the railroad station and walked to the police station.

"Can I help you?" Sue asked as Bev entered the station.

"Is Sergeant Garrison here?"

"No, ma'am," Sue answered, "but he'll be back in a few minutes if you want to wait."

Before Bev could answer, Mark walked through the door. He was surprised to see her in Riverside. "What brings you to the country?" he asked, smiling and extending his hand.

"I have a favor to ask," she said as he led her to the break room.

"Coffee?" he offered as he poured himself a cup. She refused. "How can I help?"

"I need to locate a man who was just paroled from R.C.I. His name is Wayne Burroughs. He might be in Bloomington. Can you help me?"

Mark sensed a note of urgency in her voice. "Are you hanging out with ex-cons these days, Bev?"

"No, it has something to do with Bob Archer, but I'd rather not go into the details just yet."

"I'll do what I can."

"Thanks, Mark. Will you call me?"

"Yep."

When Bev got home, her phone had two messages from George. Bev ignored the messages. As she was changing into shorts and a tee shirt, Mark called. He had information from a friend at R.C.I. who checked release records for Wayne Burroughs. Bev was right. Burroughs had gone to Bloomington. The address he had given was a boarding house. His parole officer was a woman—Sandra Johnson. Bev called the number Mark gave her.

"Wayne Burroughs is living here, but if you want more information, you'll have to come down here to get it. I don't discuss parolees over the phone,"

Sandra Johnson said curtly.

The bus trip to Bloomington was just under six hours. The town was big-
ger than Riverside, but still had the air of the country. Bev had forgotten how
flat Illinois was. She would have to stay overnight since the next return trip
wasn't until the morning. A large Mobil station served as the Bloomington Bus
Station. The gas station attendant inside did double duty as a ticket agent.

"I need to make a local call," Bev said to the agent.

He shoved a phone across the counter to Bev. She called Sandra Johnson.

"Walk across the street. I can see you from where I am. I'm in the Mercan-
tile Building on the second floor, office 202."

"Hi, I'm Bev Hudson," she said, extending her hand.

"Sit down. What's your interest in Wayne Burroughs?"

"Wayne Burroughs is a friend of my brother's. I promised that I'd look him
up when I got to Bloomington," Bev lied.

"If you're not going to be straight with me, lady, you can get back on the
bus. You came to Bloomington looking for Burroughs. I saw you get off the
bus. Now, what's your interest in Burroughs? If he gets into trouble, I get into
trouble, understand?"

"Sorry. I don't want to get him into trouble. I just need to talk to him about
another inmate at R.C.I. He really was a friend of my brother, by the way." Bev
let herself down into an old leather chair in front of Sandra Johnson's cluttered
desk. "Mind if I sit?"

"No, go ahead. Burroughs is living in a boarding house with his girlfriend.
He tells me he has a job. I hope he's being straight." She pulled some waste
paper out of the basket next to her desk and sketched a map to the boarding
house. "Don't disappoint me," she said as she walked Bev to the door with a
look that said, "Goodbye."

Lousy job, thought Bev as she stepped out into the sunlight. A hotel sign
caught her eye as she turned toward the boarding house. It was an old building
with a wooden porch that sat high off the sidewalk. Several older guests were
sitting on wooden slat chairs. At the top of the steps and across the porch was
a double door with leaded glass inserts. Inside, the lobby looked like a grand
reception room, which had been dusted by Father Time. A bell sat on the
counter. A ring summoned the clerk. "May I help you?"

"May I see a room, please?"

"Sure, follow me." The clerk led Bev up one flight of red carpeted stairs,
slightly worn on the edges. The steps to the third floor were roped off. The

first door was opened and Bev walked in. The clerk clicked on the lights. The room was clean and the air was fresh. Bev reserved the room for the night. She left one overnight bag on the bed and walked back to the front desk to complete the transaction.

Her handmade map to the boarding house was very clear. It was about four blocks from downtown. House numbers were prominently displayed next to the front door. The house had been proud in its day, but now it was humbled by age. Little maintenance had been done on either house or yard. It was evidently divided into separate living areas, but there were no names on any of the doors and no directory at the entranceway. Bev knocked on the door nearest the front entrance. A small boy answered the door. "Is your mother home?" Bev asked.

"Ain't got a mother," the boy said.

"Are you home alone?" she asked, hoping he wasn't.

"None of your business. Ain't supposed to talk to strangers."

A man in stained cotton pants and a sleeveless undershirt shuffled to the door. Bev was sure he looked older than he was. "I'm looking for Wayne Burroughs."

"Don't know a Wayne Burroughs."

"He just moved in. I understand he may be living with a woman. This is the address I got from his . . . friend."

"You mean the skinny guy upstairs. Don't know about him."

"Thank you," Bev said as she turned toward the stairway.

As she reached the top of the stairs Bev noticed that a door was partly cracked. As she approached the door she could see through the room and into a bedroom where two people lay naked on top of the bed. They appeared to be sleeping. She quietly closed the door and knocked. After a brief commotion a slender man came to the door in a pair of Levi's. "Yeah?"

"Wayne Burroughs?"

"Who wants to know?"

"I'm Bev Hudson. I'd like to speak with you. May I come in?"

"What about? I'm busy."

"About R.C.I. I'm Billy Hudson's sister."

Burroughs opened the door and motioned for her to come in. "Get dressed," he yelled to the door leading to the bedroom.

"Sorry if I came at a bad time."

"It's okay. I guess you know I just got out. I'm catching up on a few things."

"I need to speak with you about what was happening while you were at R.C.I.," Bev began.

"How much time do you have?"

"This is about a man named Harley."

"Yeah, old Harley. What a character. Hard to figure. What trouble is he in?"

"No trouble that I know of, but before we talk you should know that I am not on official business of any kind. I don't plan to record what we say and everything you tell me will be kept confidential."

"This sounds serious. Okay, sister, go for it."

Bev told Burroughs what she knew about the envelope transactions. His face grew very intense. She told him that several people had reported changes in Harley's behavior after he started receiving the envelopes. She wondered how well he knew Harley and what he had observed.

"You want something to drink—a beer or something?"

"No, thanks." She had images of the kitchen sink and passed on asking for a glass of water.

"Bring some chips and a beer," he shouted to the bedroom door, then sat in a chair across from Bev.

No one dressed or undressed ever entered the room and no chips or beer materialized as long as Bev was there. She did hear activity in the next room, but it sounded more like someone shifting in the bed. He motioned for her to sit in the sofa opposite the chair, and then talked for several hours. It was a story he was eager to tell to someone willing to hear.

Burroughs and Harley were friends. There were only two inmates on Death Row. The other man was scheduled to die in several weeks. Harley could stretch it out for awhile in the courts. Burroughs was assigned as orderly in their section. His job was to assist the guard with meals and keep the section clean. He also did the laundry for the Death Row inmates. When he was working the floors, he spent time talking to Harley. He liked him in spite of his reputation as a psycho. He talked about Harley a lot to Billy Hudson when he saw Hudson in the rec room. When Hudson asked him to have Harley place Dr. Archer on his visitation list, he didn't ask any questions because he felt sorry for Harley. He didn't have any visitors. Burroughs thought it would be good for Harley to have someone on his list, especially a doctor since he was always complaining about pressure in his chest. Billy told him the envelope would help the pressure, so Burroughs didn't think twice about passing it through. He and Harley had fun suckering the guard. Sometimes Burroughs passed it through on his floor mop. Other times, he just put it under the paper coffee cup. At times, Burroughs was reluctant because he didn't want to screw up his own parole, but Dr. Archer told him that Harley would have to continue taking what was in the envelope if he wanted to feel better. It worked. Harley told him that as soon as he started taking what was in the envelope, he felt better.

"In fact," said Burroughs, "the change in Harley was unbelievable. I wanted some of this stuff for myself, but Billy said he couldn't get any more from Dr. Archer."

"How did Harley change?" Bev interrupted.

"Completely," said Burroughs. "When we first met, Harley was a son-of-a-bitch. The guards were scared of him whenever they had to take him to the doctor or to the visitor's room. He seemed like a man who hated the world and had no conscience. Then, after I started passing the envelopes to Harley, I noticed a slight change. Harley thanked me for something. I don't remember what. It don't matter. For Harley, this was a big deal. Any kindness on his part was strange. And it continued. Within several months, Harley was asking everyone about their health, their families. He took a genuine interest in other people. Your brother laughed when I told him about the changes in Harley."

"He wants something. Watch and see," Billy said.

"I didn't think so. Then Harley began seeing a minister. When he would come back from the visitor's room it looked like he had been crying. His eyes were red and his beard was soaked. When he told me that the pain in his chest was gone, I wrote it off to the envelopes. Some kind of aspirin, I thought."

"Did you tell my brother all of this?" Bev asked, wondering why Billy had not told her more.

"Sure. It was unbelievable. He even wanted to talk to me about Jesus Christ. That's when I figured he had gone over the edge. Here's this psycho killer who was scaring the heebie-jeebies out of the guards, and he wants to tell me about Jesus Christ."

Burroughs continued his story about Harley until late into the evening. Bev was hungry, tired, and totally brain-fatigued. She interrupted Burroughs and offered to pay for pizza for him and his friend. He agreed. She left fifty dollars on a table next to the sofa, got up and thanked him for talking with her. As she turned to leave, Burroughs asked her why she wanted to know about Harley. "I'm studying human behavior," she lied, "and heard that Harley had undergone a significant change."

"You got that one right, Darlin'," he said, "you got that one right."

Bev slept fitfully in the old hotel room. It wasn't easy for her to sleep in a strange bed, no matter what she had on her mind. The room was quiet and there didn't seem to be anyone else on her floor. The only noise was occasional traffic under her window. She rose early, dressed, and walked to the gas station. The bus left on schedule and Bev sat back for six hours of reflection on what she had heard. Judy would not have left for school yet. She called Judy on her cell phone.

"Hello."

"Judy, this is Bev calling. I left a message on your phone last night to let you know that I'd be out of town. Hope you got it."

"I did. Thanks. Are you home?"

"I just got on the bus. I'll be home in about six hours. I'd like to walk in the morning. I've got news."

"I'd like to walk, too. Obviously, you haven't seen this morning's paper. The prisoner Harley died last night of a heart attack. It made the front page. You can catch up when you get home. See you in the morning."

Bev was on overload. Any more input about this Bob Archer issue and she thought she would explode. She remembered a relaxation technique she had learned in graduate school. With her eyes closed she imagined warm water pouring slowly over her head and running down her naked body. She breathed in deeply through her mouth and exhaled slowly through her nose. In a few minutes, she was relaxed and quickly slipped off to sleep.

It was 2:00 p.m. when she switched buses for home. She picked up a paper at the station. The front page had a small article about Harley. He was found in his Death Row cell dead of a heart attack. A brief biography recounted his horrible life. No mention was made of unusual behavior changes toward the end of his life. The prison doctor noted that he was surprised by the heart attack since it seemed as though the prisoner had fully recovered from a previous heart condition.

After a shower and nap, Bev resumed listening to the Harley disk. Bob Archer acknowledged everything that Wayne Burroughs had told her. Thus far the stories told by Bob, Pastor Dressler, Wayne Burroughs, and the prison doctor were in sync. The only other people who could verify the strange events in Harley's final months were the prison guards. Bev could not implicate her brother by discussing the envelope transactions with anyone at the prison.

Somehow the liposome that Bob had gotten to Harley had caused a significant change in his personality and had reversed his heart condition. Then when the gene therapy stopped, Harley returned to his original state. The mutation of gene 15105 had some effect on behavior and physical health. The implications of Bob's discovery were immense, but still unrefined.

Bev finished listening to the Harley disk and wished that Bob could have known the rest of the story. He had no way of knowing that withdrawal of the liposome would result in a reversal of Harley's condition. This was the information that he was searching for. The reversal confirmed that the mutant gene was effecting the behavior and health of those who were sampled. By logical extension, that meant every human being.

Her imagination was working overtime. It wasn't possible to draw such sweeping conclusions. Surely there must be an explanation for Harley's mood swings and health remission. Bev placed the Harley disk into the filebox and thought about where she should go from there—back to the narrative disks or to the disk with the number 323412115. She decided to do nothing for the moment.

10
The Fall

Judy knew that Bev was on to something and was eager for their morning walk. She changed into her walking clothes and headed for Bev's apartment. On the way to the door she noticed her Bible lying where she had left it after Bible study. The class notes were still slipped into Genesis, chapter three. For some reason, like Bev, she was stuck on the passage that Pastor Dressler had read from chapter five. She stopped in the hallway and read the passage again. All of her life she had heard references to the image of God. She knew what that meant and she also understood how the disobedience of the first couple had historical consequences for everyone, but this passage from Genesis five put a new perspective on the issue of sin. The first couple had been created in the image of God, but their children had been created in the image of their fallen parents. Two images? Why? Did something happen to the image of God in the second generation? Why? And what? She decided to make an appointment with Pastor Dressler.

Bev was ready when Judy arrived. They were both energized for a walk and kept up a good pace. The long bus rides had interrupted Bev's conditioning routine. "Would an extra fifteen minutes mess up your schedule?" she asked Judy.

"No. I'll be okay," Judy replied. They passed by the grocery store and kept walking. Bev brought Judy up to date on the Harley case. It was obvious that Judy was upset about the deepening involvement of Bob in a matter that was moving rapidly from unethical to illegal. Her uncertainty about the cause of Bob's suicide was fading.

Judy didn't want to go upstairs when they finished walking, so Bev went up to her apartment and got the backup disks. She gave the box to Judy and asked that Judy hang on to it. She agreed. Both women were uncomfortable about their roles in Bob's discovery, but neither could put a finger on what was at the root of their discomfort.

Judy called Pastor Dressler from school and set up an appointment to see him at 4:00 p.m. She didn't go into detail, but told him that she needed to follow up on the Bible study of Wednesday night. Scott Dressler was delighted. He was a good Bible scholar and felt that helping people understand the Bible was a vital part of his calling as a pastor.

When Judy arrived Dressler was talking on the telephone. He waved her in and pointed to one of two chairs in front of his desk. He didn't like a desk between himself and his visitors so he came around to the front of the desk and sat on the other chair facing Judy. Judy refused coffee. "You have a question about our study on Genesis three?" he began.

"Not Genesis three. I understand the Fall and the consequences of the Fall. My question is about Genesis five."

"We haven't gotten to Genesis five, Judy. You're about two weeks ahead of me, but what is your question."

"You made a reference to Genesis five, verses one to three. You pointed out that the children of the first couple were born in the image of the first couple, not in the image of God. I have always been led to believe that all people were created in the image of God."

"I wish that were so," Dressler replied. "God would have wanted that. God intended for all creation to be established in his image, the image of perfection and holiness, but our ancient ancestors changed all of that by choosing to follow Satan rather than God. When they made that choice they altered the image in which they were created."

"They altered the image, or God altered the image?"

"Actually, God altered the image. Reread Genesis three, Judy. As a consequence of their Fall into sin, God changed the rules of the game. The serpent was cursed, condemned to crawl on his belly, and told he would eat dust all his life. He was also set in opposition to humans. The woman was made subject to the man, and her desire for the man would result in painful childbirth. The man caused the ground to be cursed so that food would come only as a result of hard labor, and the end will be death—dust to dust. An unmentioned consequence of dying is aging, disease, and so on. These are the effects of sin. Immediately after God laid these heavy burdens on his first couple, he banned them from the tree of life so that they wouldn't live forever in this fallen condition."

"So the next generation of people were different than the first couple."

"The children of the first couple bore the scars of their parents' behavior. And so do we. The consequences of the original sin are still passed down through the generations."

"I've heard that before, Pastor, but how does that happen? Is there something in the physical makeup of people that changed?"

"I don't know the physiology of it, Judy. That's for God to know. I doubt that we'll ever really know how God altered the second generation. We can only see the results. That may be a question we'll have to ask when we see God face-to-face."

"The results are what you refer to as the 'effects of sin'—hard labor ending in death, desire ending in painful childbirth, aging, disease, and so on?"

"Exactly. Is that helpful?"

"Yes. I don't know how I missed the point before, Pastor. Thanks for setting time aside for me. I'll see you Sunday and again on Wednesday."

"I appreciate your faithfulness, Judy, especially after what you've been through."

"My faith has been a great help, Pastor Dressler."

On the way home, Judy couldn't keep her mind off of her conversation with Pastor Dressler. Then she thought about the Harley affair. It seemed impossible that Bob could have been so deeply involved in his work and able to keep it from her. Bob was not an outgoing person. He seldom spoke of his work, but to have been so far outside of the parameters of his profession and not send some signals, especially to his wife, was difficult for Judy to understand. Bev made it clear that Bob put her brother Billy, Wayne Burroughs, and Harley at great risk. Burroughs was now out of prison and Harley was dead, so there was no further risk for them, but Bev's brother could get into trouble if it became known that he had regularly passed envelopes to Wayne. Bev was between a rock and a hard place. Bio-Gen knew about the disks. If they ever got the disks, Billy Hudson's activities would come to light. If Bev and Judy held onto the disks, they would be in trouble. At the least, Bio-Gen wanted some return on their investment in Bob. At the worst, if they became aware of Bob's decision to do human trials without approval, they could lose their contract in the Human Genome Project, which was worth millions of dollars. Judy could see that the stakes were high and growing.

Bev looked at the disk with the nine-digit number. She was not eager to read its contents after the Harley disk, but she knew that time was running out and that she wanted to read it all before she returned the disks to Bio-Gen. She slid the disk into the drive.

11
Barbara Arnold

Bobby was the best thing that had ever happened to Barbara Arnold, and now she was losing him. The minute the purple spots reappeared in her mouth, Barbara knew that it was back. Her reprieve was over and it was now only a matter of months before she would die. The best thing that she could do for Bobby was to call her mother. The clinic had approved putting her back on the cocktail, but that only deferred the inevitable. Her mother had agreed to take the baby when the time came.

It was clear to Bev that the nine-digit number was a social security number. How could she identify the person associated with that number? Her thoughts turned again to Mark Garrison. He had helped her before. She would ask Judy to contact Mark and get help. Apparently, Bob had done another human trial with 323412115. In his narrative he noted that she was diagnosed with full-blown AIDS. Bev called Judy.

"How would you like to give me a hand with this project? I'm running against the clock and need your help. George will not let me continue to ignore his calls."

"How can I help?" Judy asked.

"Bob did another human trial with someone who has the social security number 323412115. The subject had full-blown AIDS. I need to put a name with the number, and an address, if possible."

"I don't have any idea where I'd get that information. Social Security won't release it, I'm sure."

"What about Sergeant Garrison in Riverside? He helped identify Harley."

"I'll give him a call. Better yet, I'll drive out to Riverside and talk to him." Judy really didn't want to get involved in this, but she could not refuse Bev. And something inside of her wanted to see Mark Garrison again.

"The sooner, the better, Judy."

"I'll do it today." She took a chance and drove to Riverside without calling. Sue greeted Judy as she walked into the station. After pleasantries, she walked

Judy to the break room, then retrieved Mark Garrison. "Hi!" Mark greeted with a pleasant smile as he swung into the break room. "Want a donut or coffee?"

"That stuff will kill you," Judy replied.

"Not as quickly as the stuff I cook," he rebutted.

He looked rested and happy, Judy thought. She envied him.

"What's up?"

"Bev Hudson is still working her way through my husband's disks. Apparently Bob did some trial work on a subject, but only mentioned the person by their social security number. Bev wants to identify the person by name and make contact. Can you make the match?"

"I'm not sure. It's not the same as a state prison number or fingerprints or a license plate. This is a federal I.D. I worked with an agent of the Bureau once and we got to be fairly good friends. I'm not sure where he is now, but I can try to call him. It may take a while."

"Time is something we don't have. Bev's supervisor is pushing her to return Bob's disks. There's a lot at stake here."

"You're not getting yourselves into something, are you?"

"I'm afraid we are," Judy confessed. It felt good to be talking to Mark. She felt she could trust him.

Mark saw the tension in Judy's face. He was immediately attracted by her vulnerability. He wanted to help her, but he didn't know what she and Bev had gotten into. "I'll do what I can. I know that it might be too soon after Bob's death, Judy, but would you be interested in having dinner or seeing a movie some night? If I'm off base here, just tell me."

"I'd like that very much, Mark. Perhaps when you call with the name, we can discuss it. Right now I've got to get to school." She wanted to get away as quickly as possible. The thought of seeing another man had not occurred to her, but she could be comfortable with Mark Garrison. She needed time and space to sort out her feelings. She turned and left, perhaps too abruptly.

From school she called Bev with the news that Mark would help.

Bob had done it again. It was clear from the disk marked 312412115 that Bob had done a second human trial. As soon as Judy got the identity of the subject, she would have to make contact to get the whole story. Bob's trial with 312412115 had the same result as his trial with Harley. The subject was a woman with full-blown AIDS. She presented to Bob with Kaposi's Sarcoma. She had nothing to lose by participating in Bob's experiment, and was willing to take the same liposome therapy that had worked with Harley. After several months, the woman experienced amazing improvement. During the trial, Bob's monthly examinations of the woman revealed a complete remission of Kaposi's and an increase in white blood cells. Her appetite and ability to handle food improved. In fact, her lifestyle changed dramatically. Living on the fringe of society, the woman apparently was a drug addict who leveraged her body for drugs. Shortly after beginning gene therapy, she stopped using drugs without withdrawal symptoms and expressed remorse over her lifestyle. Bob attempted to counsel her, but when she asked about making amends with God, he discontinued. Bob didn't summarize his experience with Barbara Arnold. The case was still active when he died.

Bev hadn't finished auditing the undesignated narrative tapes. Perhaps Bob concluded his trials of Harley and 312412115 there. She couldn't imagine that he would have committed suicide without knowing the results of his work.

Bev had worked through lunch and was hungry. She got up, stretched, and fixed a tuna salad sandwich. Normally, she avoided potato chips, but she had gotten a bag of kettle-cooked chips at the Deli, so she emptied it onto her plate along with a dill pickle. After pouring a glass of skim milk, she sat down at her kitchen table for dinner. Fortunately, it was a cold dinner. The phone rang as she sat down.

"Bev, I just got a call from Mark. He was able to get the identity of the person Bob studied," Judy said.

"Great. I finished listening to that disk today. It was déjà vu after Harley."

"Her name is Barbara Arnold. She lives in Richmond, Virginia. If you have a pencil, I'll give you her address."

Bev wrote down the address and the women hung up with a pledge to walk the following morning. After dinner, Bev reserved a flight through the Internet to Byrd Field, Richmond, Virginia.

The Budget desk clerk handed her a copy of the rental contract and a map of the Richmond area. "Your keys will be in the car," she informed Bev.

It took twenty minutes to drive from Byrd Field to downtown Richmond. Barbara Arnold lived in a narrow row house in the Fan District that looked out of place among the restored houses on either side. It was obvious that the Fan district had gone through several generations. Some of the houses had been restored to their time of glory. Others, like Barbara Arnold's, showed harder times. No one answered the door when Bev rang the bell. She decided to sit in a fifties-style metal porch chair and wait. Once there had been a porch swing on what was a stylish wooden porch. Now the porch swing sat disconnected from its chains at the end of the porch. After several hours of observing the passersby, Bev concluded that the neighborhood had gone yuppie.

Just as she was deciding to get something to eat, a young woman appeared on the sidewalk walking towards her and pushing a stroller. Bev dismissed the possibility that this was Barbara Arnold. Bob had not mentioned a child. As she approached the house, she yelled out to Bev, "Hi! Are you waiting for me?"

"Barbara Arnold?"

"The very same. What's up?" She lifted the stroller onto the porch and hoisted a tiny baby into her arms. "Meet Bobby," she said as she handed the baby to Bev.

Unaccustomed to babies, Bev did the expected thing. "He's beautiful," she said. She meant it. The baby's eyes sparkled. He was well fed and focused his eyes on Bev. "How old is he?"

"Six weeks," Barbara Arnold answered proudly.

"He's big for six weeks. Your husband must be proud." Bev was exploring.

"I wouldn't know," Barbara said, answering Bev's question. Bev felt like asking whether she knew who the father was, but bit her tongue.

"Who are you? Apparently you know me, but I don't think we've ever met, have we?"

"No. We haven't. I'm Bev Hudson. I'm a co-worker of Dr. Bob Archer."

"Where is Dr. Archer? He hasn't called or come for several months. I need to see him badly."

"I'm afraid that I have some bad news. May I come in and talk?"

"I have to feed the baby, but we can talk while I feed him. You can help if you don't mind."

Bev put a few groceries in the kitchen cabinet and refrigerator while Barbara Arnold gave the baby a bottle. "You aren't breast feeding?" Bev asked, then realized how stupid her question was. The purple spots on Barbara's lips were clearly Kaposi's. She couldn't breast feed her baby without risking an HIV infection. She wondered whether the baby was born HIV-positive, but didn't ask.

"I have AIDS," Barbara admitted, "but don't worry. You can't get it from casual contact."

"I know," said Bev. "I'm a biologist."

"Then you can help me like Dr. Archer helped me?"

"No. I can't. Dr. Archer was conducting an experiment, as I'm sure he explained to you. The bad news is that Dr. Archer died and his experiment died with him. The reason that I came to see you is to get more information about what Dr. Archer was doing."

"He was an angel. He cured my AIDS—for awhile, that is. Now my sores are back and I'm getting weaker. I'm afraid that I'll have to give up my baby."

"Why don't you start at the beginning and tell me how you came to meet Dr. Archer and what has happened over the past year. I have some of the scientific details, but I need to hear your story. If you like I will go out an get some Chinese and we can talk right here."

"I'm not hungry, but if you want to get something, go ahead. I'll be here when you get back."

Bev called a Chinese restaurant and ordered enough for both women, but when it was delivered, Barbara didn't eat. She put her son on a blanket and sat on the floor of her living room. The house was barely furnished, but neat. The kitchen was old, but clean. Barbara Arnold was obviously not a yuppie, but she was not Bev's idea of a druggie either. Bev wondered if she had more income than a public dole. At some point, the girl had been pretty. Her hair was brushed and clean. The red coloring was mostly grown out and revealed a natural light brown. With a little makeup she could still be attractive. AIDS had taken her desire to eat and she was as thin as a rail. The purple sores of Kaposi's circled her mouth and were probably in her mouth. Her legs were shapely and exposed in brief shorts. The buttons on the front of her loose blouse were unbuttoned so that when she bent over her breasts were exposed. She didn't seem to care. Sitting cross-legged in yoga fashion on the floor, she motioned to Bev to sit in the only chair in the living room. Bev would rather have been on the floor than in the overstuffed, stained chair, but she sat down cautiously on the edge. Barbara lit up a cigarette and began her story.

"I met Dr. Archer at a Hayseed concert in Chicago. I was a roadie with Hayseed for about a year when my HIV went full-blown and the sores started around my mouth. Dr. Archer was backstage after the concert with the group when they fired me. When you have the sores, everyone knows what's going on. It wasn't so bad. I was getting very weak and not eating. I couldn't do the work, but it was humiliating. Willard—the lead singer—was the first to see the sores. He really got pissed. He ranted and raved and made a big scene. I don't know why he got so upset. I wasn't doing it with anyone in the band. Anyway, he booted me. I saw Dr. Archer hanging around. I didn't know that he was a doctor. I figured he was a fan. He followed me out of the hall and asked me if I would like to get something to eat. It wasn't like I had somewhere else to go. He was a really nice guy. We talked for hours. He told me that he was a doctor and that he might be able to help me. He never hit on me. I mean, I looked better then than I do now. He said that he had an experimental drug that he would like me to try. I agreed. I had tried every other drug."

"By your accent, I assume that you're from Richmond. When did you come back here?"

"Right away. I saved some money and got a bus ticket to Richmond. My brother owns this place. He's loaded. Works for the cigarette company. He's going to fix this place up and unload it. He told me I could stay here as long as I wanted, but that he would be working on it while I'm here. He keeps making excuses for not working, but I know he doesn't want to make a mess for the baby and me. He's a great brother. I love him a lot. He doesn't put me down like my parents. He comes by every day. You'll probably get to meet him."

Bev slipped off the edge of the chair onto the floor. She moved closer to Barbara. "Is this too tiring for you, Barbara? Would you like me to come back tomorrow?"

"No. It's okay. Before I left Chicago, Dr. Archer met me again and gave me a small thing like a gel capsule. I took it with milk. Ugh! As God is my witness, I started feeling better that same day. I couldn't believe it. The sickness in my stomach went away and I actually wanted to eat something. He stayed with me the whole day and went out and got some avocados. I hadn't had an avocado for years, but for some reason I was craving them. It tasted so-so, and was hard to eat with the sores and all, but afterwards I felt really good. I expected for it to run out the other end, but it didn't. The next day I talked to my brother and he told me about this place. Dr. Archer gave me some money and I came here."

"Could you tell me about Bobby?"

"He's my life. He's not HIV-positive, you know. They tested him at the clinic. I couldn't believe it. Some of the babies are and I expected with my luck that he'd be sick, but he's not. I have to be real careful with him. I can't breast feed him and I have to keep the house and myself clean for him. It hurts that I can't kiss him on the mouth. Sometimes I want to kiss him, I love him so much, but I wouldn't do anything to hurt him."

"What about his father? Didn't you have AIDS when you were together? Obviously, he didn't use a condom."

"His father doesn't know anything about Bobby. We were only together once. After I got here I called Dr. Archer where he worked. He came to Richmond and checked me out, then gave me another pill or whatever. He came every month. In no time, I was feeling like myself again. The sores disappeared. I gained weight. I looked great. I even started wearing makeup again. I thought that I was cured."

"What about the baby?"

"I'm getting there. You'll have to excuse me. I run on. I haven't had anyone to talk to since Dr. Archer was here except my brother. Anyway, I wanted to do it. You know what I mean?"

"Yes." Bev wondered what she must seem like to Barbara. Suddenly she was feeling very removed from a large segment of society.

"I had decided not to do drugs or booze anymore. They messed me up. Now I had a second chance. For some reason that I will never understand, I wanted to go to a church, so I did. When I got there, I looked at the people going in and I went back home. I would have stood out there with the clothes I had on, so I got a dress. Want to see it?"

"Sure." Barbara brought out a summer dress of blue cotton material with small white stripes running from top to bottom. It was simple and modest. She also brought out a pair of sandals that looked as though they had only been worn a time or two.

"Goodwill, but almost new. The next Sunday I went back. After church I drank coffee with the people and met a very nice person. He walked me home. I was feeling great. Even my sores were gone. Over the next months we got to know each other. I hadn't had a real boyfriend since I was a kid. I couldn't believe my luck. Over and over again I told God how sorry I was about my life. I really think he listened. One night this guy came to my place. I could smell booze on him. He was coming on to me and I wasn't in the mood. Anyway, we did it and I never saw him again. He never came back to church and I never heard from him. It was like he disappeared from the face of the earth. Dr. Archer was great. He let my cry it out. So, it's over and now I have Bobby. Bobby is a story, too."

"Are you able to tell me the story?" Bev could see that she was getting tired.

"Sure, I'm okay. I've been with my friends when their kids were born and I had decided not to have kids. I didn't want to go through all that pain. The thing of it is—when Bobby was born there was no pain. I mean it. No one believes it, but the truth is that I only knew he was being born because all of a sudden I was flooded with water. Then, presto, here comes Bobby. I called my brother and he took me to the clinic. They kept telling me that they could ease the pain. I kept telling them that I wasn't having pain. No one believed me. Bobby came out like an angel, no HIV or anything. It was a miracle. When I told Dr. Archer, he just smiled. He always believed me. I miss him a lot. How did he die?"

"He took his own life."

"How? Why? He was a young guy."

"That's what I'm trying to find out. That's why I'm here. I'm trying to put the pieces of the puzzle together. Is there anything that you can tell me about Dr. Archer?"

"Just what I've already told you. He stopped coming a couple months ago. He didn't leave any of his pills with me. He brought one whenever he came. Then he just stopped coming. Now everything is back."

"Tell me about that, Barbara."

"This week the sores returned, then the diarrhea. I stopped eating when the diarrhea came. Now my stomach is sick again. I knew that it was too good to be true. I know that when the sores come, the end is close. My Mom has agreed to take Bobby. She loves Bobby. He'll have a good home with her. She hates me, but she loves Bobby."

"I'm sure she doesn't hate you, Barbara," Bev said, hoping she was right. "She may be disappointed in your circumstances, but mothers don't stop loving their kids."

"You couldn't prove it by me. After I moved back to Richmond it took a month for her to come and see me. Even then things didn't go very well. Now all she knows about me is what my brother tells her. Frankly, I have stopped going to church. I don't have the desire for it. I'm trying not to go back on drugs, but I can tell you, the urge is there. It's all I can do to settle my guts."

"Are you taking medication for the AIDS?"

"That's the other thing. While Dr. Archer was coming I didn't have to take anything. When I went back to the clinic this week for my cocktail, they thought I had died. They have never ever heard of anyone going off the cocktail and living this long. I'm back on the cocktail now and it's like it was before. I know that before long I'll be in the hospital again. Look, I'm getting tired. Could we call it off for tonight?"

"Sure. Is there anything I can do for you before I leave?"

"Yeah. Give me your address and phone number. Let me know what happened to Dr. Archer, okay?"

"Do you need money, Barbara?"

"No. I'm okay."

Barbara stood with Bev at the door until the cab came. She gave her a hug and said goodbye.

12
The Burglary

Bev knew that something was wrong as soon as she stepped out of the cab. The timer in her apartment was set to turn the living room light on at 6:00 p.m. and off at 11:00 p.m. when she was away. When she stepped out of the cab her apartment was dark. She climbed the stairs to her apartment. The door responded normally to her key and swung open. Reaching into the room, she turned on the hallway light. Her heart sank. Everything was in disarray. Quickly, she turned off the light, closed the door and rushed out of the building. The grocery store was closed, but there was a public phone at the service station at the end of the block. Bev ran to the phone and called Judy.

Judy knew that something was very wrong by Bev's heavy breathing. They agreed to meet outside the grocery store as soon as Judy could get there. Bev watched the store from a distance. No one came or went. She was relieved when Judy's Escort pulled up in front of the store.

"Did you call the police?" Judy asked as Bev approached the car.

"I don't think there's anyone there," she replied. "I was afraid to go in alone. Would you go in with me?"

The women entered the apartment cautiously. Again, Bev flipped on the hallway light. They could see part of the living room from the hallway. There were no sounds coming from inside.

Bev lived simply. She had no interest in jewelry or furs or anything that a thief might sell. Her electronic equipment consisted of old stereo components and a computer system. She rushed to her computer nook. Bob's disks and her CPU were missing. Closet doors and drawers were open, contents were disturbed, but nothing else seemed to be missing. Bev would have to go through everything to be sure.

"I think that we should call the police," Judy said as she sat down in the kitchen.

"We can't call the police," Bev responded.

"I don't understand."

"The disks, Judy, the disks." Bev had never been short with Judy, but she

86

was tired from her flight back from Richmond and was not herself. She immediately regretted her tone of voice. "I'm sorry, Judy. I shouldn't have spoken that way. What is on Bob's disks is very incriminating—for Bob, and now for me. Professionally and ethically, I should have alerted Bio-Gen when I first realized what Bob was up to. If Bob's trials become general knowledge, N.I.H. will drop Bio-Gen like a hot potato. The Human Genome Project is Bio-Gen's bread and butter. Without it, they'll go down the tubes. The Genome Project protocol is very tight. Lot's of people are suspicious about genetic science so the subs are very careful to dot all the I's and cross all the T's."

"I'm not entirely clear why anyone would steal the disks," Judy said.

"I'm probably to blame," Bev speculated. "I didn't keep my commitment to George, my supervisor. He made it clear that Bio-Gen was anxious to get the disks. I haven't been answering his calls. At first, I was certain that his interest was just a matter of housekeeping and a gap in the backup sequence. Now, I'm not sure. I can't imagine that George or anyone at Bio-Gen for that matter is aware of what's on the disks. I'm sure they think that it's routine data from Bob's project."

"We don't know who took the disks and we don't have the expertise to check it out. If we can't call the police officially, would you agree to call Mark Garrison?"

"Only if he would help us unofficially."

"I think that it's a possibility, but let me make the contact. He asked me out. I think he has a personal interest."

"Could you call him now. I'm very uncomfortable staying here tonight without someone being on our side."

"You will stay with me tonight. Agreed?"

"Agreed."

"I'll call Mark and see if he can come over. Did you ever mention to George that you made an extra copy of the disks?"

"No, he has no idea that there are disks at your house. I'll need to use those disks and your computer until I can get Aaron to replace my CPU, if it's okay with you, Judy."

"Fine."

Judy called Mark at the Riverside station. He was gone for the day. She got a home phone number for Mark Garrison from 411 and called him there. Finally, a break. Mark answered and agreed to come right over. Judy didn't tell him the details, just that Bev had been burgled and they needed his help.

He climbed the steps to Bev's apartment two at a time. Without knocking, he opened the door and walked into the living room. The women were surprised at his entrance. "Is everyone okay?" he asked.

"We're fine, Mark," Judy explained. "I'm sorry if I startled you."

It took about an hour to bring Mark up to speed on all that happened, including Harley, Barbara Arnold, and the break-in. He listened attentively without committing himself. "Will you help us, Mark?" Judy asked.

"I don't think you know what you're asking," he said. "First, tell me exactly what it is that you are expecting from me."

The women weren't prepared for his question. They didn't know whether they wanted Mark to "solve" the burglary—a solution that would only plunge them deeper into the Archer affair, or whether they wanted protection and advice on how to proceed with their review of the disks. They opted for the latter, but they also needed to solve the burglary to know how much they were at risk.

"My advice is to go to the city police and report the burglary."

Judy felt betrayed. She was sure that Mark would help them, but she was beginning to understand what she had asked him to do. If he got involved in their situation, he would be complicit in the whole mess. She wasn't sure she wanted to put him in that position.

"At this point, Bev, you haven't broken any laws that I know of. Not turning over the disks is an internal matter for Bio-Gen to deal with. Your position and possibly your reputation are at risk, but there is nothing with which you could be charged. We're not dealing with a violation of law as far as the disks are concerned. Failure to report this burglary, however, is another matter."

"What is your take on the burglary, Mark," Judy asked.

"Who would have an interest in these disks?" Mark asked.

"Certainly Bio-Gen, N.I.H., and Barbara Arnold. Harley is dead." Bev answered.

Mark followed Bev around the apartment, observing the things that were out of order. "Was anything taken other than the disks and CPU?"

"It doesn't look like it."

"Check carefully tomorrow and let me know. In the meantime, my take, assuming that nothing else is missing, is that someone had a specific interest in the disks. That would put Bio-Gen and the rest under a cloud."

"But they don't know what's on the disks."

"As far as you know."

"How could they?"

"Is there anyone involved in Dr. Archer's activity that could have made contact directly with Bio-Gen?"

Bev thought immediately of Barbara Arnold. She was desperate to get more of the liposome. Would Bob have told her about Bio-Gen? Not likely, but who else would have made contact?

Bev decided not to inventory her things until morning. Instead she packed an overnight bag and went home with Judy. Mark left without a commitment to investigate the burglary, but Judy felt that he would help them.

"Stealing the disks is a bit extreme, don't you think?" Judy asked as they drove home.

"I should have seen it coming," Bev replied. "George's messages were sounding pretty tense. I let it go too long. He wasn't eager to let me take the disks home in the first place." She hated the thought of calling George to report the theft.

George didn't lose his temper often, but he was irate about the burglary and demanded that Judy come to the lab the following morning. He would arrange to have Bio-Gen management at the meeting. This Archer matter had gotten out of control. He expected Bev to make a full report of the contents of the disks and cooperate with the city police in the investigation of the burglary. Bev asked George whether he had notified the city police. He hadn't. She suggested that they not be notified until after her report tomorrow. When he heard what was on the disks, he might feel differently about getting the police involved. George agreed.

Bio-Gen was a small company. It had gone public when they won the contract with N.I.H. as a Human Genome Project subcontractor. A CEO, COO, and Treasurer ran the company. All three were assembled with George in the conference room when Bev entered. They stood and greeted Bev. Bev felt like she was facing a parole board.

George set the stage. He quickly summarized Bob's work, his suicide, the discovery of the disks, Bev's assignment, and what he knew of the burglary. Bev was impressed with the amount of detail that he shared about the Archer affair. It struck Bev as odd that he didn't mention the missing disks. He was probably expecting Bev to do that. She was grateful that he didn't mention her delinquency in returning the disks. In fact, the tone of the meeting was much less tense than she expected. The executives asked about the status of Dr.

Archer's project and how Bio-Gen planned to continue his work. If they only knew, Bev thought. She gave a fictitious summary of the contents of the missing disks as if Bob had continued on course. George assured them that they would be able to continue Dr. Archer's project from the disks in their possession even if it meant duplicating his work of the past fourteen months. That seemed to satisfy them. The meeting was concluded. George asked Bev to meet him in his office after he and the executives returned from lunch.

"I don't know what you're up to, Bev, but let's be clear about one thing," George said when they were alone in his office. "I didn't believe your report for one minute. It was pure fantasy. There is something in the missing disks that caused Dr. Archer to kill himself, and I believe that you know what that something is, don't you?"

Bev didn't know this side of George. He had played politics with the management team, but now he was venting his real feelings. Bev was unsure about how to proceed. If she told George the truth, she was finished and Bob was disgraced. And if George told the management team the truth, the company was in jeopardy. "I'm not ready to make a detailed report of the disks, George. They were stolen before I finished reading them," she lied.

"Since there are no longer any disks, you can report on what you already know. I expect your report on my desk in one week. After you have concluded your report, you will remain on the Bio-Gen payroll until your own project is complete, then you will report to H.R. for outplacement counseling. Any questions, Bev?"

"You mean I'm fired?"

"I mean exactly what I said. And if you fail to complete your project, you will receive no outplacement help and no transitional reimbursement."

Bev was furious. Not at being fired. Not at George. She had screwed up and she knew it. She was furious at herself. Why had she invested herself so heavily in Bob Archer? Subconsciously, she knew the answer. Bob's discovery was important even if his methods were unacceptable. He had put people at risk without full disclosure. He had violated scores of mandatory procedures for human trials. But he had discovered a common mutation in Gene 15105 and a remedy. And he had resolved both behavioral and physical problems in his two human subjects, at least while they were receiving gene therapy. "My own project has been done professionally," Bev said. "Will outplacement counseling include reference letters?"

"That will depend on how well you cooperate, Dr. Hudson. First I want to see the report on Dr. Archer's work on Gene 15105."

On the way to the bus stop, something was disturbing Bev. Something that George had said did not resonate with her. She couldn't put her finger on it, but she was unsettled.

She rode the bus, then walked six blocks to Judy's townhouse. Judy had given her a key to the townhouse until Bev moved back to her own apartment. She opened the door and was accosted by Kelly. At once, he settled down and followed her deliberately to the kitchen. After a snack, she popped a disk into Judy's computer. She had now read all but one of the narrative disks. This was the final narrative, then she would scan the unread data disks. In time, someone would have to read the data disks in detail in order to duplicate the liposome remedy, but that would be someone else's task.

The final narrative disk was the beginning of an assumption. Bob assumed that all humans had the same mutation in Gene 15105 . . . That was it. George had referred to Bob's work on Gene 15105. That was what was disturbing Bev after their meeting. Bob's assigned project was not on Gene 15105. Gene 15105 was the defective gene that Bob discovered in the course of his project. Bob's assigned study gene was 314. As far as Bio-Gen and George were concerned 314 was the only gene that Bob was investigating. George would have no way of knowing about 15105 unless someone with access to the missing disks had told him.

She decided to discuss George's slip with Judy and Mark, but first she had to finish reading Bob's assumptions. Obviously, his assumptions would be incomplete. Both human subjects changed after Bob's death. At the time of his assumptions, the subjects were undergoing gene therapy with amazing results. Since the missing base pair on gene 15105 was apparently universal, Bob had to determine its effect on human subjects. Both subjects had reversed lifetime behavior patterns. Harley had been a psychopath, Barbara Arnold was a drug user and prostitute. Neither showed any redeeming characteristics. Both had serious health deficiencies—Harley with his heart, Barbara with her AIDS. Both behavioral and physical problems changed dramatically after beginning gene therapy. During the time of Bob's observations, which included physical interviews with Harley and physical examinations of Barbara, neither subject experienced *any* physical illness. Previous conditions disappeared—totally. Their character patterns also reversed. Harley, who was known at R.C.I. as a bad person, became considerate and compassionate. Barbara, whose life was on the skids, gave up drugs and prostitution without any withdrawal symptoms, then delivered a baby without labor pain. To the surprise of everyone who knew them well, they both developed a conscience and sought to get right with God. Harley developed a relationship with the prison chaplain who led him through the process of confession and absolution. He was baptized only several months before Bob died. Barbara Arnold, who had been baptized as a child and had attended Sunday school, became curious about God. Bob's narrative downplayed the spiritual connections, and broad-stroked the changes in Harley and Barbara with the following statement: "Both subjects have experienced perfect health, socially responsible attitudes, and religious curiosities."

Bob would never know that after his death, when gene therapy was curtailed, both subjects reverted back to their previous conditions. A supplemental assumption would need to be added to his research notes: "Improvements from gene therapy is not spontaneous or lasting when therapy is ended." In other words, therapy must continue for improvements to be lasting.

Bev slid the last disk into its place in the filebox. She had now read all of the narrative disks, including the Harley disk and the Barbara Arnold disk. She had not read all of the data disks. The only thing that she wanted to extract from the data disks was Bob's procedure for developing the liposome. That would be her next project, but it would have to be done on her own time. If she wanted help from Bio-Gen in getting another job, she would have to return to work and her project. She decided to tell Judy about Bob's assumptions, then return to the lab on the following day.

Judy returned home at her usual time with a cloth bag filled with school papers to be graded. *Teachers are unsung heroes,* Bev thought as Judy came through the door. Knowing that Judy would be tired, she had prepared a spinach quiche for their dinner. Judy caught the smell as she entered the house. "You're an angel," she said to Bev. "I never could get Bob into Quiche's. What a treat."

"It's back to the salt mines for me tomorrow," she said to Judy. "I'll have to sleep in my own bed tonight."

Everything seemed normal at Bio-Gen. Bev's lab and office were as she had left them, or so it seemed at first glance. But when she sat down to make some phone calls, she noticed that her office tools were not in the same order. Her stapler was on the opposite side of her tape dispenser. She checked the contents of her desk drawers. She was neat, but not that neat. Someone *had* gone through her desk. Maybe they had done the same in Bob's office. It was locked. Bob and Bev had exchanged keys when they began sharing a lab. Bob was notorious for forgetting his keys, so Bev was his backup. This was strictly against company policy. Bev turned Bob's key into his office door. No luck. The locks had been changed. This confirmed Bev's suspicion about George. She remembered his slip about gene 15105, which she had intended to discuss with Judy and Mark.

After changing into lab clothes, she turned on her computer and set up her work for the day. George came into the lab about 10:00 a.m. Bev wasn't surprised to see him. "We've decided not to report the theft of the Zip disks to the city police since they are routine research data which would have no particular value to anyone outside of Bio-Gen."

Bev knew George was hiding something. If he didn't already have the stolen disks, and if he wasn't going to report the burglary, he would have hired someone to find them. He would not treat them so casually. They contained pure dynamite. She decided not to mention her desk or Bob's locked office. She was already on thin ice with George and Bio-Gen and needed their reference to get other work. Anyway, by now they were aware of Bob's discovery and were taking steps to control the damage. George left without pleasantries. Bev called Judy at work and arranged for her to invite Mark over to Bev's apartment in the evening. She then called Barbara Arnold.

13
Sin Gene

"Hello," a man answered.

"Hello. Barbara Arnold, please."

"May I ask who is calling?"

"A friend. With whom am I speaking?" Bev asked.

"This is Barbara's brother."

"My name is Bev Hudson. I came to see Barbara several days ago. Could you put her on the telephone?"

"I'm sorry to tell you, Ms. Hudson, that Barbara died in the hospital yesterday. Did you know of her condition?"

"Yes, I know that she had AIDS, but I'm surprised she died so quickly. I just saw her several days ago and she didn't seem like she was near the end."

"We didn't think so, either. Actually, she bled to death internally."

Bev expressed her condolences and said goodbye. Internal bleeding was not consistent with Kaposi's Sarcoma or any of the other opportunistic diseases that invade the body when the immune system is down. And Barbara was not near death just days before. Bev was alarmed. All of the main characters in Bob's trials were now dead, including Bob.

Mark preferred to meet Judy and Bev at Riverside Park. He was following a policeman's intuition and putting some distance between himself and the women. They hadn't heard from him since the burglary and were not sure whether he was going to help them. Skipping their walk, the women agreed to meet with him early. Both were sitting on a picnic table when Mark's unmarked police car pulled to the curb. As he approached, Judy wondered if he still wanted to take her out. Nothing further had been said about the prospective date. "Have you been waiting long?" he greeted with a smile.

"No, we just got here, Mark."

It was obvious that he had already had donuts. White powder had fallen on his collar. He was clutching a plastic Dunkin' Donuts coffee mug. "I'm sorry about being so protective the other night. I'll help you as much as I can, but it

94

will have to be on my time off. I assume that's why we're here."

"I want to bring both of you up to date since the burglary," Bev interjected. She shared her suspicions about Bio-Gen, including George's reference to gene 15105. "Barbara Arnold is dead. She died of internal bleeding. I was surprised when her brother told me about her death. It hasn't been that long since I saw Barbara. That she died suddenly of internal bleeding is inconsistent with her condition."

Mark was holding his microcassette recorder while Bev talked. He stopped her long enough to change tapes. Somehow he'd have to con Sue into transcribing his tapes on her own time. He hadn't crossed that bridge. "It sounds like you think Bio-Gen has the tapes."

"How else would George know about 15105? And why would they have gone through my desk and secured Bob's office?"

"The way you describe the situation there are high stakes for Bio-Gen. What would you have done? I'm not saying that they stole the disks. There may be other explanations for what they know. Where was Barbara Arnold on the night of the burglary?"

"I don't know. She died two days later, so I'd say she was probably in Richmond."

"You said that she was desperate to get whatever it was that Dr. Arnold was giving her, right? Did she know where you live?"

"I gave her my telephone number."

"It's a library visit away from having your address. An old military buddy of mine is living in Richmond. I owe him a call. I'll get back to you," Mark said to Bev.

Bev spotted her bus at the city building and excused herself. She was already late for work at the lab. Judy hadn't said much during their visit. She was trying to read Mark. "Do you think Bev is in any danger?" The thought had bothered her ever since the burglary.

"Not now that the disks are gone. Unless someone is uncomfortable with what she knows, or what they think she knows. The backup disks at your house put you at some risk, too, you know."

Judy hadn't considered herself at risk. Bev and Mark were the only two people that knew she had the backup disks and they weren't going to tell anyone.

"Judy, I asked you the other night whether we might have dinner or see a movie. Have you given that any thought?"

"Yes, I have. I'd like that very much."

"Great!" He seemed genuinely pleased. "How about Friday evening? Is there anywhere special that you'd like to go?"

"You pick it. Call me. Right now I've got to get to school." She gave his hand a squeeze and got up from the picnic table. Together they walked to her car. Mark held the door while she got in.

Mark closed the door to the interrogation room and called his friend in Richmond. Ted Tubb was a former military policeman, who had left law enforcement when he was discharged. Now he was a real estate salesman with listings for the high-end properties on the West End of Richmond. Mark and Ted kept in touch, but not as much as either would have liked. "It's good to hear from you, Mark. What's up?"

Mark explained the situation regarding Barbara Arnold. He wanted to know where she'd been on the night of the burglary, and whether there was anything unusual about her death. He told Ted as much as he knew. Ted was pleased to help. Real estate was down because of high interest rates and he had time on his hands. He promised to get back to Mark.

Bev promised Judy that she would go with her to Bible class. Pastor Dressler was going to cover the fourth chapter of Genesis. Going to Bible study wasn't as high on Bev's list as Judy's, but she needed the diversion. Scott Dressler was setting up the class when the women arrived. He greeted them while he worked. Pastor Dressler did his research in the original languages. He liked working in Hebrew and Greek. It gave him a sense of involvement with the word. Every time he re-studied a part of the scriptures, he felt he learned as much or more than his students did. Today's lesson was about the inherent nature of humankind after the fall of Adam and Eve into sin. Cain and Abel were the star characters.

As usual, Pastor Dressler began the class with prayer and a review of the previous week's lesson. He recounted the fall and the consequences for creation, with emphasis on human consequences. Then he introduced the class to Cain and Abel. It was a familiar story for Bev and Judy. Judy was uneasy about the inherent evil in Cain's nature. The contrast between Adam and Eve as they were created and Cain seemed striking. Pastor Dressler spoke about original sin as a condition of the human race since the Fall. As a Christian Bev never questioned the veracity of the scriptures, but as a scientist, she had been trained to think in terms of cause and effect. Dressler had told the class, "Since the Fall the very nature of all creation is changed." Bev wanted to know more about the physiology of original sin.

"Changed how?" Bev asked, trying not to sound skeptical.

"Humans now experience the effects of sin," he answered.

"I know," said Bev. "Disease, rebellion, death—all of these, but what is the mechanism that triggers these changes? We know that God created all things with a word that placed into motion the stars, the earth, living things in a complex array of matter. Something in his arrangement was changed by the Fall. What exactly was it?"

Scott Dressler was not a scientist. He was a brilliant pastor and scholar, but he wasn't equal to Bev's scientific question. "I can't give you the scientific answer that you're looking for, Bev. God didn't give scientific answers. The Israelites needed to know which God to worship. They weren't seeking scientific answers. That came later—with the Greeks. Perhaps someone else in class can help." No hands were raised.

After class Bev and Judy stopped at Denny's for dessert. As before, Scott Dressler came into the restaurant. This time he was alone so the women invited him to their booth. "Hope I didn't put you on the spot," Bev said.

"No problem. I've been on the spot before," he smiled as he sat down. "I've never really considered the physiology of original sin."

"Is it possible that God not only changed the nature of creation after the Fall, but that he also effected humans genetically?" Bev asked.

Judy came alive. All of a sudden Bev's probing seemed to take direction. She thought she knew where Bev was headed.

"Anything is possible with God, I guess," Dressler replied. He finished his coffee and excused himself. "See you Sunday?"

"Yes," said Judy. Bev's mind was somewhere else.

"Are you thinking what I'm thinking?" Bev asked.

"Is it possible that Bob stumbled onto the 'sin' gene?" asked Judy.

"That's one way to put it, I guess," said Bev. "I would rather think that Bob has discovered the 'sin' therapy."

Sue was at her desk when Mark came into the station with his regular bag of Dunkin' Donuts. He sat on the edge of her desk as he prepared to deliver his speech about the extra-curricular transcription. "I have a favor to ask," he said directly. "I'm doing some work for a friend on my own time, and you know how much I hate to write reports." He was holding his microcassette tape in his hand so that Sue could see it.

"I get it, Mark," she said, her face frozen. "And what do I get in return for this unofficial assignment?"

"My enduring love and respect."

"Doesn't cut it," she said, still expressionless. Mark thought he was going to have to type the paperwork himself.

"Would money get the job done?" Mark was desperate.

"Have all I need," she replied. "But, I'll tell you what."

"What?"

"I'm going to think of something very expensive that I've always wanted. I'll let you know what it is." She looked very serious.

Mark laid the tape on her desk, not knowing that he was being teased. She picked it up and kissed it. "One thing, Sue," he said. "The stuff on this tape is confidential. It could put you at some risk. Strictly between us, okay? Still want to do it?"

"Your price tag just went higher," she smiled. "Seriously, Mark, I'm behind in my department work and I don't have a transcriber at home. It may take a while."

"It can't take too long, Sue."

He took his donuts into the break room and poured himself a cup of coffee. Just as he arrived at his desk, Sue buzzed his phone. It was Ted Tubb. "I didn't expect to hear from you so soon, Ted."

"It didn't take long to learn that Barbara Arnold was not at home on the night of the burglary. She was in Chicago."

Mark couldn't believe his ears. "Chicago?"

"I checked the airlines. United had a Barbara Arnold on a fast round trip to Chicago. They don't have descriptions of passengers so I don't know whether it was your Barbara Arnold. It's not a strange name. I'll keep checking, but I thought that you'd like to know."

"Anything on the cause of her death?"

"Not yet. I'll get back to you on that."

Mark checked the Richmond phone directory. There were seventeen Arnold's in Richmond. It was probably a coincidence, but he knew Ted. Ted was thorough. He'd get the job done. Mark would have two gifts to buy when this was over.

Ted checked the obituaries. A listing for Barbara Arnold had already been printed in the previous day's paper. The viewing had been held the same night. An informal graveside committal for family only was scheduled for 10:00 a.m. It was 9:15 a.m. Ted ran an electric shaver over his face and raced to the cemetery. The casket was in position over the grave. Ten folding chairs had been lined up on green indoor/outdoor carpeting under a tent roof. Two men in black suits were standing nearby as several cars pulled up on the cemetery road. Ted watched the brief proceeding from his car. The small group conversed briefly after the service, then left. Ted approached the men in black suits. They assumed, as he hoped they would, that he was a family mourner. He milked the mood. "I can't believe she's gone," he said.

"We're very sorry for your loss. Were you a relative of Miss Arnold?"

"Yes, a distant relative. The rest of the family had a problem with her lifestyle, but she was a sensitive and caring person," Ted said, hoping for some insight from the men. "She's the first person I've known to die of AIDS. I suppose that causes special problems for your work."

As professionals, the men were reluctant to discuss personal matters regarding the deceased. "We have to take precautions," they replied. "But your family member didn't die from AIDS."

"No?" Ted was all ears.

The two men let Ted know that the conversation was over by excusing themselves and returning to the cemetery office.

Ted knew that most AIDS patients were indigent drug users. He assumed that she was a patient of a free clinic. The County Health Department clinic closest to the address listed in the obituary was his first stop after the internment. Ted struck pay dirt. An underpaid clinic aide fell for Ted's line and gave Ted the name of the EMT that treated her at home. Ted looked him up in the phone directory. He was at home. Barbara Arnold collapsed and died in her home. She was lying in a pool of blood under the lower part of her body. Bleeding was apparently from the rectum.

Ted checked the county records to see whether the death certificate had been filed. It hadn't. He returned to the clinic. The clinic physician on duty had pronounced Barbara. The cause of death was AIDS. No autopsy had been requested. The physician would not discuss the case with Ted.

Ted went to the Internet. He couldn't believe how much information he found on AIDS. Nowhere did he find internal bleeding as an expected result of Kaposi's Sarcoma. Ted was getting conflicting input. The physician had written AIDS as the cause of death. The men at the committal service had said that she had not died of AIDS. The EMT had said she bled to death. The Internet did not show internal bleeding as an expected result of Kaposi's. That didn't mean that Barbara Arnold didn't die from some other opportunistic disease, but within the week before her death she seemed to be strong, and she may have been well enough to fly roundtrip to Chicago. The pieces were not coming together.

Ted returned to the cemetery. He wanted to talk to the person who prepared the body. This time he was on the level with the director. "I'm a friend of a friend of Barbara Arnold. Barbara was involved in a confidential clinical trial. Her death was sudden, AIDS notwithstanding, and it is important to know the circumstances. This information will be held in the strictest confidence." The director was cooperative. Ted was amazed. He thought that he should try the truth more often.

The funeral director took Ted to the prep room and introduced him to the technician. Ted was surprised to be shaking hands with the same man who had been at the committal—the one who told Ted that Barbara had not died from AIDS. "Hi, again," Ted said as they shook hands. The director excused himself. "At the committal service for Barbara Arnold you made the comment that she had not died from AIDS. I need to know why you said that."

"Because she was soaked in sweat, her lower extremities were blue, and the EMT that brought her in said that she was burning up with fever when they arrived at her house. Her death could have been the result of any number of things, including poisoning."

"What was the cause of death?" Ted asked.

"I'm not a doctor. I'm told the cause of death was complications resulting from AIDS. I don't sign death certificates. You'll have to speak to the doctor."

Ted returned to his real estate office and called Mark. "Here's the dope, Mark. The cause of Barbara Arnold's death is in question." He went on to explain all that he had learned. Simply put, she may have been in Chicago on the night of the burglary. She may have died from AIDS, but both issues were wide open.

Mark decided to discuss Barbara Arnold's symptoms with Doc Spencer.

Dr. Spencer was at the diner where they had agreed to meet. Mark extended his hand as he slid into the booth. Marge took Mark's lunch order as he and Doc Spencer exchanged opening pleasantries. "I'm helping a friend with a situation, so what I'm going to ask is off the record, Doc. Are you up on AIDS?"

"Not really. We don't get much of that around here and I didn't deal with it before I retired. I've seen a few cases as coroner, but Riverside has been lucky on that score. Ask your question and let's see where it goes. We're not speaking of you, I assume?"

"No. I'm not sure which is best, to be a candidate for an STD, or involuntary abstinence."

"You should find a nice girl, Mark."

"Believe it or not, Doc, I've got a date for Friday!"

"Not with the AIDS patient, I hope?"

Mark laughed. "No, the AIDS patient is dead. That's what I need to talk about. I'm not sure it was AIDS that killed her." Mark described Barbara Arnold's condition as he had heard it from Ted.

"It's a crap shoot without the body and an autopsy report. I agree that Kaposi's Sarcoma, as I understand it, leaves another trail. The appearance of the deceased at the time of death would make me suspect that she did what some AIDS patients do—took her own life. The symptoms are consistent with various kinds of poisoning: Blue skin, high fever, sweating, internal bleeding—maybe aspirin overdose."

"Could this be homicide?" Mark asked.

"You're the cop," Dr. Spencer said as he got up to leave.

Mark finished his lunch and returned to the office. He would call Judy after she got home from school.

14
Sin Therapy

Ever since the Bible study and the discussion with Pastor Dressler at Denny's, Judy couldn't stay focused on her work. The possibility that Bob had discovered a sin gene and a remedy occupied all her thoughts. Pastors are sworn to confidentiality, so Judy knew that she could trust Pastor Dressler to keep their conversation confidential. She would make an appointment to see him after school. Pastor Dressler agreed to see her on the way home.

Scott Dressler was with another member when Judy came to the office. His secretary had left for the day. The door opened a crack when Judy knocked and Dressler spoke to her softly, "Please have a seat at the secretary's desk, Judy. I'm running over a little."

Judy sat down and organized her thoughts. How much should she discuss with Pastor? Would he take her seriously? Just then Judy heard the outer door to Pastor Dressler's office open and close. His meeting was over. He opened his inner door and invited Judy into the office. "I've been expecting you to call, Judy," he said as he motioned her to sit down.

"I'm not sure I understand," she replied.

"It's not easy to lose a husband."

"I'm dealing with that, Pastor. In fact, I'm a little confused. I had always thought that if Bob died, I would come apart. I haven't. I'm doing fairly well. The townhouse is quieter than I would like, but that started long before Bob died. I guess I got used to being without Bob just over a year ago. I've been so busy with school and with the circumstances following Bob's death that there hasn't been much time to grieve, or to do whatever widows do. I don't like the sound of the words *grieve* or *widow*."

"I thought you had come to talk about that," Scott said, somewhat perplexed.

"No, actually, I didn't."

"Now I'm at a loss. How can I help you, Judy?"

"Bear with me, Pastor, I have a strange story to tell you. Do you remember our conversation the other night—after Bible study, at Denny's?"

"Please refresh me."

"We were speaking about the physiology of original sin."

"Yes, I do. I thought about it quite a bit after I left, but I thought it was an academic discussion. Is there more to it than that?"

"Quite a bit more. In fact, I believe that my husband was doing research on that very issue at the time that he died and may have made a discovery of some importance."

"I'm surprised that Bio-Gen is interested in matters of this sort."

"They're not. That's part of the problem. He was working on the Human Genome Project, but his work took him in another direction and he got in too deep. He took some risks that could have had serious consequences. It may explain why he took his own life. I'm not sure about that. What I need to discuss with you is whether his work is consistent with what we believe as Christians."

"I'll need to know more than what you've told me, Judy."

"What I'm telling you is strictly confidential, Pastor Dressler. It could have serious consequences for Bev Hudson and Bio-Gen if it becomes general knowledge."

"You know that I'm sworn to confidentiality."

"Thanks. Bob discovered a gene defect that is common to every human subject he tested. I don't know the scientific details. Bev does. As I understand it, he was not able to determine the effect this defect had on his subjects because it was universal. The only way to discover its effect was to correct it and watch for changes in the subject. Bob was good in his field. In fact, he did discover a remedy for the defect. Where he made a bad turn was that he decided to pursue the issue on his own, including human trials—without authorization from Bio-Gen. Without naming names, he administered the remedy to two people. The effects were remarkable. Both subjects experienced improvements in health and behavior. Both wanted to get right with God. These were extreme subjects in every aspect of human life and while they were undergoing treatment from Bob the effects of sin as you described them in class seemed to disappear. After Bob died and the treatment ended, both reverted back to their former states. They, too, have since died. I know this sounds ridiculous, but Bev has listened to Bob's working disks. She agrees that something very important and phenomenal has happened."

Scott was thoughtful. Surely there was a logical explanation for Bob's discoveries, but he didn't have it. A sin gene and a scientific remedy for sin were certainly out of the question. Only God could alleviate sin and its consequences. Scott's whole life had been committed to that belief. God's remedy was final and lasting and came through repentance and faith. If a remedy for sin could come from a bottle, the church had little to offer. The implications of Bob's work were far-reaching, but not just for Bob and Bio-Gen. "I don't know how to respond to you, Judy," he confessed. "There is no provision in the Bible for a man-made remedy for sin. That isn't to say that many haven't tried to overcome their sin, or its consequences, by their own means—but never successfully. Check out Romans 6:23 and Ephesians 2:8-9. People have placed their trust in miracles before, Judy, and been disappointed. The Shroud of Turin and the current interest in near death experiences have distracted Christians from the spiritual and the divine. It is there that the sin remedy is to be found, Judy. Please don't let Bob's scientific discoveries steer you away from the spiritual."

Pastor was right, of course, Judy conceded. Bob's discovery was another in a whole history of attempts on the part of people to do what only God could do. She felt better. She'd try to put Bob's work in a different perspective. She thanked Pastor Dressler and headed for home. Mark's call was waiting on her answering machine.

Judy took Kelly out on the leash, then left him at the bottom of the stairs as she went to her bedroom. She shut the blinds at the front of her townhouse and slipped out of her clothes. For the first time since Bob's death, she luxuriated in a warm scented bath and read school papers while she sipped on a glass of white port. When she finished with the papers, she added more hot water to her bath and called Mark on her portable phone. She hoped that he had called about their Friday night date. She wasn't in the mood to talk about Bob.

"Hello," Mark answered.

"Hello, Mark. It's Judy Archer."

"Hi, Judy. Thanks for returning my call. I have some information on the Barbara Arnold situation."

"I'm not in the mood, Mark. Could we talk about it tomorrow night?"

"You want to talk about Bob on our first date?"

"You have a point. What is it you want to tell me," Judy conceded.

"Barbara Arnold may have made a round trip flight to Chicago on the night that Bev's apartment was burgled. And her death is not necessarily the result of AIDS. Ted has done some good work."

"What's your take?" she asked.

"I wouldn't rule her out as a suspect in the burglary. According to Bev,

Barbara Arnold admitted that she was desperate for what Bob was giving her. She had access to Bev's address. It was a matter of life and death for her. And she was street smart. As of this moment, there are two possibilities—Bio-Gen and Barbara Arnold."

"Where do we go from here?" Judy asked.

"It depends on how far you and Bev want me to push, and what you want to do with the information when you get it."

"If Barbara Arnold took the disks, what would she do with them? She's dead and certainly no threat to anyone. If Bio-Gen took the disks, they would have to destroy them or go out of business. Only Bev could tell us whether the disks have value to another scientist or lab."

"We'll discuss this with Bev after our date Friday night," Judy said.

15
First Date

"Speaking of our date—what did you have in mind?" Mark asked.

"How about something public and casual for starters—like a movie and pizza?"

"You're on," he agreed. "I'll pick you up around 6:45."

"Later." Judy rinsed herself off under the shower, dried herself and carried her empty wineglass to the kitchen. She poured another glass of wine and sipped it while Kelly curled up at her feet. Like a schoolgirl anticipating her first date, she was already planning what she would wear—tight jeans and a pull over blouse with a sheer bra. Her feelings for Mark were slightly uncomfortable considering the short time since Bob's death. They were tempered with guilt, something she needed to deal with by telling herself the truth. Guilt over what? She would work on that.

Scott Dressler thought about what Judy had told him in his office. It was bizarre. A sin gene. A sin therapy. Strictly science fiction stuff. It conflicted with his faith system. Only God could fix the sin problem. This had been hammered into his head since childhood. It was the central message of every sermon he had ever preached. Grace alone, faith alone, Scripture alone. The effects of sin were part of God's punishment against the condition of sin. Only God could pardon the sinner from the consequences of sin, and even then, the solution would only be partial until the Consummation. There could be no remedy for the effects of sin except from God. Original sin was more than a broken gene, but Bev raised a good question. What is the physiology of original sin? Scott instantly thought of one of his professors at the Seminary. Professor Schmidt held the Simon Chair of Bio-Ethics. He would be the person to call.

Gene Schmidt was out of the state for a few days, but would be at the Bio-Ethics in Religion Conference in Chicago on Monday, according to his secretary. Dressler got the information about the conference and made an appointment to have lunch with Dr. Schmidt on the first day.

106

• • •

Judy almost gasped when she opened the door for Mark who, like a good policeman, showed up promptly at 6:45 p.m. He was wearing a maroon pullover
and khaki pants with loafers. He looked perfect in every way. His short hair
had been trimmed, and his musk cologne was detectable, but not overwhelm-
ing. Her heart had not beaten against her chest this way since her prom night.
She didn't think that she would ever feel this way again. Wearing a pair of white
flats without stockings, tailored jeans, and a sheer bra under her sleeveless white
blouse which had several manageable peek-a-boo angles, Judy hoped Mark would
find her attractive. Her blonde hair was pulled back over her ears and tied in a
ponytail in the back. Strategic dabs of White Shoulder said, "I'm yours." From
the way Mark took her inventory, she was pleased with the result.

"Promise me, Judy. No talk of Bob tonight," Mark implored.

"I promise," she said as they got into his unmarked police car.

"I've never been on a date in a car with so many radios," Judy remarked. "Is
this your only car?"

"Sorry, yes," Mark said. "But you'll be safe. There's a shotgun in the back
seat."

They decided on pizza first since they were both hungry. Mark drove to a
pizzeria in Riverside. True to her word, Judy avoided the subject of Bob. Since
they had never talked about anything except Bob there was a lot of ground to
cover. By the time their deluxe pizza was delivered they had covered their families of origin and the highlights of their childhood's. Although neither was a
regular drinker, the beer menu was tempting with over sixty micro-brewed offerings. Mark ordered a dark ale and Judy had a Miller Lite. Neither had checked
the movie listing so Mark stepped outside of the pizzeria to buy a newspaper.
They decided on a prison film by Stephen King, *The Green Mile*. It was showing
in Riverside. As if magnetized, their hands grasped easily as they left the pizzeria.

The movie ended at 10:05. As they walked to Mark's car, they discussed the
spiritual dimension of the film and decided that King's spiritual side was curious indeed. They couldn't agree on the spiritual message. Mark had to work on
Saturday. Judy didn't. He suggested that they stop at Riverside Bowl for a few
games. Judy had never bowled and had an image of bowling alleys that she
didn't want to share with Mark. Since he seemed enthused, she agreed on the
premise that he would be patient with her. Mark looked forward to teaching
Judy how to bowl. The alley surprised Judy. It was well-lit, smoke free, and

orderly—not what she had expected. She didn't relish the idea of wearing a pair of shoes that had been on thousands of feet, so Mark bought her a pair of sockettes to wear under the rented shoes. Most of the patrons greeted Mark by name. He seemed well-known and well-liked, but all eyes were on Judy. They tried bowling balls until they found two that fit and headed for an open lane. Both enjoyed the contact of Mark's lessons. Judy worked her blouse for all it was worth and took longer than necessary to master the bowling technique. After two games, they left to go home.

Judy had thoroughly enjoyed Mark's company and the events of the night. She hoped the feeling was mutual. Mark seemed to be having a good time. "I haven't been on a date in a long time, Judy," he admitted. "This was very special for me."

"Neither have I," she said with a hint of regret.

"But you've been married for years," said Mark without picking up Judy's meaning.

"We didn't date much during the last years of our marriage, but I promised not to discuss Bob."

"I'd like to see you again, Judy."

"Me, too."

Mark pulled into a parking space in front of Judy's townhouse and got out of the car. He opened her door and they walked to the front door.

"I have to take Kelly out on the leash. Would you stay with me for a few minutes?" she asked.

"Of course," he agreed. He hadn't been looking forward to saying good night, because he was uncertain how to end the night. A simple kiss at the door seemed so 1950ish, yet it was as far as he intended to go on the first date. He hoped Judy wouldn't expect more.

She came out with Kelly on the leash. The dog jumped up on Mark. Judy scolded him, but Mark liked dogs and got along well with them. He walked with Judy to the grass alongside the curb where the dog did his business. Mark followed them up the steps to the front door. Judy opened the door enough for Kelly to slip inside, then closed the door again. She turned her back to the door and faced Mark with a look that said, "If you don't kiss me now, don't call me again." Mark got the hint. He gently lifted her chin and kissed her lightly on the mouth. She let the kiss happen, then put her arms around Mark's neck and pulled his mouth tightly against hers. The kiss didn't linger. Both felt heat and a hormonal rush and they backed off simultaneously.

"Thanks for a wonderful evening," Judy said as she stepped into the townhouse.

"I'll call you tomorrow," Mark promised.

Judy smiled. Mark forced himself to leave. His feet never touched the steps or the sidewalk as he returned to his car and headed for Riverside.

Scott Dressler waited in the lounge for Dr. Schmidt. They were to meet at 11:45 for lunch in the restaurant at the hotel where the Bio-Ethics in Religion Conference was being held. It was already noon. Scott wondered if Dr. Schmidt had gotten distracted or forgotten their meeting. He was, after all, one of the featured speakers at the conference. He probably wouldn't even remember Scott. Scott had only had Dr. Schmidt for two classes at the Seminary and Schmidt certainly couldn't be expected to remember all the students he had taught. The conference was open to pastors, doctors, attorneys, chaplains, nurses, and others who had an interest in hearing the latest developments in the bio-ethical field. Scott wished he had registered, but registration was closed when he spoke to Dr. Schmidt's secretary. Dr. Schmidt was to look for a man in a dark suit and clerical collar. Scott realized how ridiculous that description was at a conference attended by pastors. He looked around. He didn't see anyone else in a suit. Just as he was giving up on Dr. Schmidt, he heard his name called from behind. He turned to see Dr. Schmidt approaching him with his hand extended. "Hello, Scott. It's good to see you again. Shall we go into the restaurant?" Scott followed the energetic, elderly man into the restaurant. They were seated at a table for two.

"I didn't know whether you'd remember me, Dr. Schmidt," Scott admitted.

"Of course I remember you, Scott. You were in two of my bio-ethics classes. I seldom forget a student, although some of them have aged a bit and I have to mentally recolor the gray hair and remove the mid-life paunches to remember them as I knew them." Scott smiled. "How have you been, Scott? What are you up to?"

"I'm sole pastor of a medium-sized church and have a family. I'm still at the same church to which I was sent from the Seminary."

"Unusual," said the professor. "Many men move around. It's disturbing for the church. Glad to see that you didn't, Scott. I looked for your name on the list of participants at the conference, but missed it," he said inquisitively.

"I'm not registered. Your secretary told me that registration was closed when I spoke with her."

"Not a problem. I can get you registered. You've only missed the morning session. There are two more days of lectures."

"I'm not here for the conference, Dr. Schmidt. I have another matter that I want to discuss with you if there is time."

"I have until 1:00, then I will have to return to the conference," said Schmidt.

"First, let me say that by telling you what I'm about to tell you I'm violating the confidence of a church member. I have thought carefully about whether to share this. If the matter became public knowledge, it could hurt a lot of people. I don't have permission from my member to discuss it. On the contrary, I've been asked not to. That's my first dilemma. And I guess I'm now asking you to share my dilemma."

"The right to privacy ends when the safety of others is at stake, Scott. You learned that in my classes. If someone asks you to keep confidential a matter that places another person at risk, you have two obligations: First, to tell your confidant that you are not under any obligation to keep information secret when another person might be in danger. Second, you are under obligation to do what is necessary to help when someone is in danger, whether that means notifying the officials, seeking emergency medical help, or intervening to prevent injury. Does your situation fall into these categories?"

"In a way. Actually, much of the damage was done before I learned of the situation. Several key players are dead and others are now at risk."

"Is this a matter for the police, Scott?"

"Perhaps you can help me decide that. I'm mostly concerned about the implications it has for the church."

"Why don't you start at the beginning."

Scott set the stage. He began with the death of Bob Archer then proceeded to tell Dr. Schmidt what Judy had shared with him placing emphasis on the theory that Archer had discovered a sin gene and a remedy for the sin gene.

"What do you mean, a 'sin gene'?" Schmidt asked.

"Apparently, Dr. Archer learned that every human being has a defective gene, number 15105, which, when repaired, alters the health, behavior, and religious orientation of the subject. It seems to undo what was done after the Fall. There are several phenomena involved. First, the mutation is universal—a scientific oxymoron. Second, the remedy is transient. When the gene therapy is withdrawn, the subject reverts to his or her former condition. Third, the results of the gene therapy are common to both subjects—possibly universal. Dr. Archer experimented without authorization on two human subjects, both of whom exhibited extreme social negativity, both of whom had health problems, and both of whom were unchurched. After therapy, their behavior, health, and religious curiosity did a flip-flop and remained Edenic until the therapy ended. Now they are dead. And Dr. Archer has taken his life."

"Edenic?" asked Dr. Schmidt. "Explain, please."

"As I understand the results of the therapy, both subjects were without the effects of sin, just as God created the first couple in the Garden of Eden."

"Remarkable. Do you have any proof of this, Scott?"

"No. I have only the report of my member. Proof would be difficult. The disks on which the experimental data and assumptions were recorded have been stolen in a burglary and, as I said, Dr. Archer and his human subjects have died. I have no reason, however, to doubt what I've been told. I'm sure you can see why I felt that it was necessary to share this."

"Yes, of course, although I'm not sure why you're sharing it with me."

"Because you are an authority in the matter of bio-ethics. You can appreciate the consequences of Dr. Archer's experiment—for his company, for the scientific community, and for the church."

"There are legal, ethical, and moral consequences for his company, Scott, assuming they know about this. The scientific community will relish the thought that sin can be reversed from a test tube. As for the church, well, the consequences are apocalyptic. The core of the church's belief and teaching is that the effects of sin can only be reversed through repentance and faith. This is the message of the Bible from beginning to end. A human, scientific remedy would compromise the church's appeal and purpose. And this at a time when social institutions are doing their best to make the church irrelevant. Only the most deeply committed believers would be able to place all of their faith in the divine mystery when there is a bottle on the shelf that can deliver the goods. If what you tell me is true, Scott, we could be seeing the end of the church."

Scott wasn't yet certain why he felt the need to share Judy's story with Dr. Schmidt. Partly, he wanted to mitigate his own burden. Assuredly, he did not anticipate such an extreme reaction. Dr. Schmidt was speaking about the end of the church! "Certainly this is not the first time that human beings have sought to be like God."

"That's what got us into the sin dilemma in the first place, as you know, Scott. Believe me, I trust God and his promises. I'm just not in counsel with God. I don't know whether his hand is in this. One thing is certain, the message and means that he has given to the church will have some stiff competition if this sin remedy becomes a reality. Scott, you've done the right thing sharing this with me, but I must tell you that it is too big for me. I cannot promise that I won't discuss it with my colleagues. Do I have your permission to do so?"

Scott didn't want to get Judy into hot water. He knew that if he gave Dr. Schmidt permission to discuss the matter, he would have to reveal his breach to her. He would face that when he had to. "Yes, of course."

The two men walked silently out of the restaurant. Dr. Schmidt saw Scott to the revolving doors of the hotel lobby and said goodbye. Scott watched as Schmidt walked rapidly toward an elevator.

On the following day, as Scott scanned the morning newspaper, he was startled to read that the Bio-Ethics in Religion Conference had been cancelled.

16
The Conference

Dr. Schmidt awoke on the same morning to prepare for a hurriedly assembled meeting of denominational leaders who had attended the Bio-Ethics in Religion Conference. Other leaders would be arriving for the cloistered afternoon session. All except Dr. Schmidt were curious about the topic and the urgency.

No explanation was given for the cancellation to the participants of the Bio-Ethics in Religion Conference. A note had been placed under the door of each participant's hotel room stating that the remainder of the conference had been cancelled and offering partial reimbursement for the registration fee. Of the 121 participants, sixty-three were invited to remain for a "special" meeting to take place beginning at 1:00 p.m. The sixty-three were high-ranking representatives of Protestant and Jewish denominations. Missing were leaders of the Roman Catholic and Orthodox churches who had not attended the conference. Urgent calls went out to these leaders to join the group for the 1:00 p.m. session.

No agenda was included with the invitations. Dr. Schmidt persuaded the conference committee to make the changes based on what he had learned from Scott Dressler. Although his information was skimpy, he planned to share with the group what Dressler had told him in the hope of organizing an investigation into the matter and developing an announcement to the church bodies when the matter became public knowledge.

The special meeting was delayed until 2:30 p.m. to accommodate late arrivers. Dr. Schmidt was chairman. Media representatives were excluded from the meeting, which heightened their interest. The media, whose numbers were increasing, had already reported the cancellation of the conference. Schmidt knew that it would be impossible to keep some of the church leaders quiet after the meeting, but he was determined to keep a lid on the matter until Dressler's information had been corroborated. He was especially concerned about one representative of a Pentecostal church who was a nationally known televangelist with a reputation for the sensational.

It took Schmidt about thirty minutes to report on Dressler's information.

The hasty notes he recorded after his meeting with Dressler were fairly accurate. Without using Archer's name he described his discoveries and trials with emphasis on the ramifications for the church and its doctrine of salvation by grace alone. The room was silent as he spoke and for a few seconds afterward. There was no applause. Participants were stunned. Several leaders with multiple disciplines were asked to serve on a research committee to establish the facts. Several others were asked to form a communications committee to write a common response to the church bodies. All agreed.

As soon as discussion was opened, hands were raised throughout the meeting room. Responses were varied. Almost all of those who responded demanded verification of what until now was fourth-hand information. Some, assuming that what Dr. Schmidt had reported was true, likened the attempt to reverse the effects of sin as just another in a series of historical efforts to be like God. This attempt, like the others, would fail. Thou shalt have no other gods. There was a murmur of approval as one after another upheld the Biblically divine monopoly over human righteousness.

A representative of a church body that did not believe in the divinity of Christ and which had been heavily represented at the bio-ethics conference, applauded the work of Dr. Archer and pledged its support to continue his work. God could certainly work through science as he had already demonstrated in the medical field. Such a remedy for the effects of human imperfection should be welcomed as another advance in the general body of knowledge and human development.

The televangelist whom Dr. Schmidt suspected of being a possible security leak stood and spoke without being called upon. He would not allow the unsupported report of Dr. Schmidt to deter him from the Gospel. The church stood on the promises of the Gospel. Any substitute would prove false and must be opposed by the church at all costs. The future of the church depended on the traditional message of the Gospel.

Discussion continued until 6:00 p.m. when Dr. Schmidt adjourned the meeting urging participants to keep the matter confidential until the communication committee issued a release simultaneously to each church body. He scheduled the research and communication committees to meet on the following morning. Media surrounded participants as they left the meeting room, but nothing was released to the press, at least immediately.

Scott Dressler had no knowledge of the meeting. Although he had given permission for Dr. Schmidt to share the information, he had no idea that it would be disseminated so quickly to so many. He had not spoken with Judy or Bev about his breach of confidence. He didn't know that it would become front-page news before he could redeem himself.

David Daniel wasted no time. He ordered his team to come to Chicago. They would meet on the following morning in his hotel room. His team consisted of his business manager and his public relations manager. Both arrived in time for the morning meeting, which started with breakfast served in Daniel's room. He briefed them on the Archer discoveries and the implications for his ministry. "If this guy Archer is on to something we are out of business. There will be a mad rush to the drugstore and our supporters will leave us in the dust. We have to do something to see that this doesn't happen." All agreed that something had to be done to stop the Archer business from proceeding.

David Daniel was a fraud. He was a performer who had acquired enormous wealth at the expense of his followers. His hands-on-the-screen healing services and preaching histrionics had attracted a following of gullible, needy people who were ignorant of his personal excesses and immoral lifestyle. He would stop at nothing to keep the development of the Archer remedy from progressing.

"Who do we know in Chicago that can get to this minister and stop this thing?" Daniel asked his team.

"We'll get it done," his business manager promised.

Judy missed her morning walks with Bev, which stopped when Bev returned to work at the lab. Bev was swimming again and Judy was exercising on her Nordic equipment at home. They had not talked for almost a week. It was a good thing in a way because it had given both of them a time to clear their heads. Bev was trying to bring her project at Bio-Gen to a conclusion so that she could get on with her life. Judy was focusing on her schoolwork and life without Bob. She was hoping that Mark would call again, but it had now been five days since their date and she hadn't heard from him even though he had promised to call the next day. She couldn't know that he was in a panic. He had never fallen so completely for anyone before and was sorting out his feelings. She decided to call both Bev and Mark. After all, this was the twenty-first century. Women don't wait for men to call anymore. She would call them both this evening.

Scott Dressler was uneasy. He knew that he would see Judy at the Bible study tonight. He debated about arranging a brief meeting before the study to tell her what he had done. He left a message on her answering machine asking her to come by the church early.

Hearing a tap on his outer office door, Scott opened the door to find Dr. Gene Schmidt standing there. Dressler rose to greet him and ushered him into his office. "I wasn't expecting you, Dr. Schmidt. You were lucky to catch me at this hour. It happens that I have a Bible class in an hour and a half. Please come in and have a seat. Coffee?"

"No, thanks, Scott. I'm sorry that I didn't call in advance. I took the chance that you'd be here. I know the long hours pastors put in so I won't keep you. Things are moving very fast since our lunch meeting. I suppose you read that the Bio-Ethics in Religion Conference was cancelled."

"It was in the morning paper. What happened?"

"There was nothing taking place at the conference that was more important than what you shared with me at lunch. The conference committee decided that the church leaders present should hear your story. I told them what you shared with me, but I need for you to come to the morning session tomorrow. I want you to meet with the committee that is assigned to look into the Archer project."

Scott was alarmed. "Dr. Schmidt, this is a very sensitive matter. I told you that the disks containing Dr. Archer's research are missing. Little can be done to further the project. Public disclosure will hurt a lot of people, including the research company. I'm not sure that this should go any farther."

"It's too late for that, Scott. Denominational leaders from all over the country know about the Archer project. I have asked them to keep it confidential until the research and communication committees can get more information. I can't guarantee anything, especially with David Daniel involved."

"David Daniel—the televangelist?"

"The very same. He's a loose cannon. He was at the meeting this evening."

"Dr. Schmidt, what I told you at lunch was already fourth-hand information. The person closest to the research is Dr. Archer's co-worker at Bio-Gen. She listened to his disks. They were stolen from her apartment. She is the only person who can explain the project in scientific terms; however, I doubt she would participate in your meeting."

"Will you ask her to come?"

"I'll call her right now." Bev answered Scott's call. To his amazement, Bev agreed to speak to the research committee. She believed in Bob Archer's project.

Bio-Gen would do nothing to continue his work, but Bev had already been fired and had nothing to lose.

"She has agreed to meet with the committee," Scott reported.

"Good. I've scheduled the meeting for 8:00 a.m. in my hotel suite. I'll see you and Bev there?"

"We'll be there," Scott promised. Gene Schmidt passed Judy Archer as he walked to his rented car.

Scott held the door for Judy. He didn't know how to start telling her that he had violated one of the most sacred promises of a pastor—the promise of confidentiality, and that tomorrow her private story would become a national news item.

He skipped the pleasantries. "Judy, I have something to confess to you and it isn't easy. You swore me to confidentiality and I have violated your confidence in a big way."

Judy sat silently, waiting for Scott to continue. He wished she would say something. "Two days ago I met with a seminary professor who is an expert in the field of bio-ethics. He is in town for a conference. I knew him from my days at the seminary and respect his knowledge in the field. I told him about your husband's project. I did it because of the implications that Dr. Archer's project has for the church. I ask for your forgiveness."

"Do you think he'll keep it confidential, Pastor? It could hurt Bob's company and his reputation if it became public."

"There's more to the story, Judy. The conference that the professor was attending was cancelled in order to discuss Dr. Archer's project. By now a hundred or more church leaders know the story. They intend to dig deeper into the matter and communicate it to their church bodies when they have all the facts." Scott couldn't look into Judy's eyes.

"What can I say?" Judy said in resignation. "As for forgiveness, you are forgiven, but I wish that you had told me your plans before you went public. It would have been easier for both of us. There's nothing that can be done now except to wait for the fallout. I have to tell you, Pastor, that I'm deeply disappointed." Judy left the office and returned home.

Scott Dressler didn't expect Judy to return to his church again. He stood at the outer door of his office watching her get into her car. As she drove away, he noticed a man in a black car parked across the street. The man was looking toward Scott, but Scott couldn't make out his face. It was too early for the Bible class students to be arriving. Scott began walking toward the car, but it pulled away as he took the first steps. He returned to his office. For the first time in weeks, he moved some books from his prie-dieu and knelt in prayer.

Bev was already in Dr. Schmidt's suite when Scott arrived. There were seven in total at the meeting: Dr. Schmidt, Scott, Bev, and four church leaders with multi-disciplined academic degrees. These were men that Dr. Schmidt had worked with in the field of bio-ethics for many years. He trusted them. A continental breakfast was laid out on the breakfast bar in Dr. Schmidt's suite. Scott poured a glass of orange juice and wrapped a bagel in a napkin before taking his place in the living room. The atmosphere was informal. Scott was introduced first, but deferred almost at once to Bev who explained Dr. Archer's project in some detail. She omitted any direct references to Harley and Barbara Arnold. The group was warned that Bio-Gen would resist strongly any identification with Dr. Archer's work and might even take legal action if their name became connected with his project. Bev also acknowledged that she was scheduled to be released from the company. After her presentation there were many questions. Was Dr. Archer's work proprietary since it was done in the Bio-Gen labs, but without their knowledge? Could Dr. Archer's work be continued without the research disks? Was any effort being made to locate the stolen disks? Were his results conclusive? Bev answered each question. It was concluded that without the disks, Dr. Archer's work could not continue, and for all practical purposes the sin gene project was ended. No mention was made of the backup disks at Judy's townhouse, or of Bev's full intention to continue Bob Archer's project somewhere sometime. The meeting ended at 11:30 a.m. Bev and Scott walked together to Scott's car.

"How did this get so far?" Bev asked. Scott admitted his breach of confidence and apologized for getting Bev involved. They both agreed that the meeting was probably the end of the issue as far as the church was concerned. Without the disks, it would be impossible to continue the project, and thus any threat to the church was ended. There was nothing for the communications committee to report. Scott didn't know about the backup disks in Judy's possession, and Bev had no intention of telling him.

As Scott pulled into a parking space in front of Bio-Gen, he noticed a black car pass him and park on the opposite side of the street about 100 yards ahead of him. He said goodbye to Bev and pulled away from the curb. The driver, who had not gotten out of the black car, turned his head away as Scott passed him. In his rear vision mirror, Scott saw the car pull away from the curb and turn into a side street and disappear. It resembled the car that had been parked outside of his church the night before.

17
Murder

A note was in Judy's school mailbox when she arrived. It was a telephone message from Mark. Would she meet him for lunch? Her heart skipped a beat as she walked to the school office and called the police station. Sue answered and told Judy that Mark was out of the office. Judy left the message that she couldn't meet Mark for lunch, but wondered if he would like to come to her townhouse for dinner at 7:00 p.m. Unless she heard otherwise, she would expect him. Sue promised to relay the message.

Judy got home at 4:00 p.m., slipped out of her school clothes, and hurriedly straightened the townhouse. She hadn't dusted or vacuumed for weeks, so she got caught up on light housekeeping. Mark was a meat and potatoes man. She baked an everyday meatloaf with a ketchup topping and baked two Idaho potatoes. A tossed salad and French bread would round out the meal. She had some ice cream in the freezer for dessert. No candles or romantic music, she decided. It was too soon in their relationship for that, but she dabbed some White Shoulders on her neck just in case. Slipping into a one-piece outfit that zipped down the front, the thought occurred to her that he might not come. He had taken a long time to get back to her. She would be ready in any case.

Kelly heard Mark before he got to the door. Judy got excited when she heard Kelly's bark and opened the door before Mark had a chance to push the bell. In his hands were flowers, wine, and candy. Now she wished that she had put candles on the table. Taking his gifts, she said, "It isn't my birthday, Mark. Why the extravagance?"

"I owe you an apology. I promised to call you on Saturday, but didn't. I'm sorry."

"I hope everything is all right," she replied.

"Couldn't be better," he answered. "The truth is, I've been sorting out my feelings, Judy. It's been a long time since I've had feelings for a woman. I need to tell you right now, Judy, that I care a great deal about you." It was obvious that he had been rehearsing his speech and had to deliver it before he fainted.

Judy put the flowers in a milk vase and placed it on the table, put the candy

119

in the refrigerator, and poured a glass of wine for each of them. Before joining Mark she lowered the zipper in the front of her one-piece outfit so that a hint of cleavage was showing, then joined Mark on the living room couch. "I have feelings for you, too, Mark."

Despite her plans to omit the music, she got up to put her Amadeus CD on the player. Mozart's music stimulated her when she did housework. Perhaps it would stimulate Mark. Just as the wine and music were doing their job, the oven timer rang. "Time to eat," she said to Mark. They went into the kitchen of the townhouse and Kelly followed the meatloaf scent into the kitchen after them. He curled up on Mark's feet. His affection for Mark didn't go unnoticed by Judy.

Mark didn't disappoint Judy. There was very little meatloaf left after dinner. He had a good appetite and enjoyed her meal. "You're a great cook," he said, finishing his ice cream. He hadn't had a home-cooked meal since he had eaten with Judy and Bev. He missed that. Most of his meals were eaten at Marge's Diner or Dunkin' Donuts. They cleaned up the kitchen together.

In the living room Judy brought out some photo albums and gave Mark a history tour of the family. Mark was curious about Bob. How had they met? Why were there no children? What was their marriage like? Judy spoke openly and fondly of Bob. Mark respected that. They were sitting on the floor of the living room with photo albums spread out before them. Johnny Mathis was singing *The Twelfth of Never*. Judy hoped it wasn't too obvious. When the tour ended, she stacked the photo albums on the coffee table and pulled Mark to his feet. Without hesitation he put his arm around her waist and asked her to dance. She had never danced like this with Bob. He enjoyed line dancing, but it never interested Judy. Judy slipped off her shoes and let Mark pull her in close. She assumed the traditional dance posture, but soon let her arms slip around his waist. They swayed to the music in place allowing the touch of their bodies to communicate their feelings. They danced for almost an hour without a word. Both of them were making up for years of missed affection. Judy was afraid to look up into Mark's eyes for fear of what might follow, but when he put his hand under her chin and pulled her face to his, she had tears in her eyes. Their lips met and they were bonded. Mark had little experience with women; however, he knew what he wanted—a traditional relationship that wasn't consummated until the wedding night. He didn't know where this was leading. Judy had been married. She might want more. After a few minutes of passionate kissing, Mark pulled away.

"I should probably go," he said. "I need to cool off."

Judy loved him. She could finally admit it to herself. She had fallen in love with Mark. She was afraid to tell him for fear he would feel pressured. "Please don't wait a week to call me again."

"I promise. Judy, I have to tell you that I have very strong feelings for you. I'd like to see you often, if that's okay."

"There's nothing I'd like better, Mark." They walked arm in arm to the door. He turned her around at the door and gave her a long, lingering kiss. Without a word, he released her and left. She leaned on the inside of the door for a long time, then took Kelly out on the leash and went to bed. Sleep didn't come for hours.

When Judy arrived at school, the next morning a dozen red roses were sitting on her desk with a note, which read: "I love you. Mark." She cried.

Judy had no idea that Bev had addressed Dr. Schmidt's special committee. She hadn't spoken to Bev for a long time and decided to arrange to walk with her on Saturday. She left a message on Bev's answering machine telling her that she would come by at 7:00 a.m. unless she heard otherwise.

On Saturday morning, Judy got up earlier than usual and dressed for a walk. She drove to Bev's and parked in front of the grocery store. At the top of the stairs, she could see the door to Bev's apartment standing slightly ajar. She called from the door, but got no answer. Something wasn't right. In the city no one, especially Bev since the burglary, left his or her doors standing open. Bev should be here. She hadn't called to cancel the walk. Judy pushed the door open and stepped into the foyer leading to Bev's living room. It was déjà vu. The apartment was totaled. Judy backed out and went to her car and called Mark on her cell phone. He told her to call 911 from her cell phone and wait in front of the grocery store until he got there. The police responded to her 911 call within ten minutes and entered Bev's apartment. Judy was surprised when an ambulance arrived. Could it be that Bev was in the apartment? She assumed that Bev was gone. Judy jumped from her car and raced up the steps to Bev's apartment. A policewoman stopped her at the doorway. "Sorry, miss, but you can't go in there. This is a crime scene."

"I know that," Judy said. "I'm the one who called the police. Is Bev Hudson in there?"

"Yes, but you can't go in there," she repeated as she stepped between Judy and the doorway. "I'm afraid that she's dead."

Judy's body gave way under her. Just as she collapsed onto the floor, Mark arrived taking the stairs two at a time. He showed his badge to the police-woman. While picking up Judy, he asked, "What's happened?"

"We got a call about a suspected burglary and found a dead woman inside. We're waiting for homicide now. This place is a crime scene. You can't go in until homicide is finished. Even then, you'll need permission."

Mark understood the drill. He carried Judy to his car and held her until she was strong enough to sit up. "What happened, Mark?"

"I don't know yet, Judy, but I'll find out. Are you okay? Can you sit in my car until I get back?"

"I'll be all right."

Mark went back to the apartment and spoke to the officer in charge. No one was permitted in the apartment until the lab had finished its work and homicide detectives had completed their investigation. That could take days or weeks. The officer who responded to the call filled Mark in on some of the details. Bev was tied to a chair in the kitchen. Her throat was cut. There were bruises on her face and neck where it appeared she had been hit, possibly tor-tured. A dishrag was stuffed into her mouth. All of the blood was confined to the area around Bev, so the beating and the murder had taken place where Bev was found. The apartment had been searched methodically. Someone wanted something very badly. That was about all the officer could tell Mark. Mark was sickened at the thought of what had happened. Although he had been a police officer for years, there had been only one murder in Riverside during that time. A woman sewed a bed sheet around her stuporous husband and beat him to death with a baseball bat. Mark went slowly down the stairs. How would he tell Judy?

Judy was standing next to her car, which was blocked in by emergency ve-hicles. The grocery store owner was standing with her. "What happened," she asked Mark. She could see that he was pale and needed to sit down. "Sit in my car, Mark, and tell me what's going on."

"Bev's dead. She's been murdered. Someone was looking for something in her apartment. There is evidence that they beat her before they killed her. It may have been someone who didn't know that the disks had been stolen. I hope she didn't tell them about the backup disks at your house, Judy."

"How was she killed?"

Mark avoided the question. Judy was sitting next to him in her car. He pulled her close and held her tightly. "How was she killed, Mark?" Judy de-manded.

"Her throat was cut."

Judy hadn't anticipated that. She gasped and began to cry.

"We need to get away from here, Judy, and talk. We'll take my car. We can come back later for yours." They left in Mark's unmarked police car and went to Riverside Park. Mark stopped at Dunkin' Donuts for two black coffees. At the park, they sat silently on a picnic bench. Finally, Mark broke the silence. "I don't know what's going on here, Judy, but I think that you may be in some danger. Someone wants those disks badly and you have the only set in the universe. What's wrong with that picture?"

Judy told Mark about Scott's indiscretion and the bio-ethics conference.

"I don't understand why the church would be so upset over your husband's business."

"Who would go to the church for redemption if you can get it at CVS?"

"I get the picture. Is the church capable of doing something like this?"

"I hope not. Who knows? There are others who were desperate for Bob's secrets."

"We don't know what Bev might have said before she was killed. You know what that means."

"Not really. You're the cop. I know that this person, or these people, are desperate. What should I do?"

"Leave for awhile. Until this gets settled. We'll find a safe place for the disks and for you. Would you be comfortable moving into my place? Although my place is not very fancy, I have a guest room."

"I don't think so, Mark. Thanks for the offer, but I don't want this to destroy what we have between us and I'm not sure I could handle living in the same house with you just now."

"I love you, Judy." Mark held her tightly.

"I love you, too, Mark. We'll have to get past this, though, before we can get on with our relationship. I can't handle all of this at the same time."

"I understand. We have time."

18
Going Home

Judy wanted to stay with Mark forever. Once again, as when he told her about Bob's death, she could feel his strength supporting her.

They decided that Judy should take a leave of absence from her job and stay with her parents until Bev's murderer was in custody. Mark would put the disks in the evidence lockup at the Riverside Police Station.

Mark drove Judy to Bev's to pick up her Escort. The emergency vehicles had been replaced by unmarked police cars. Men in suits and lab coats were coming and going from Bev's apartment. Mark got more information from one of the detectives who corroborated what they had already been told. In addition they learned that Bev's answering machine had been taken. The Medical Examiner had removed Bev's body and taken it to the morgue for an autopsy.

"If they have her answering machine, Judy, they know about you. Didn't you leave a message on her machine about walking?"

"Yes."

"Let's get back to your place and get you packed." Mark followed her to her townhouse.

As they approached Judy's townhouse Mark noticed a black car parked on the opposite side of the street. After attending to Kelly, Judy called her parents. They were pleased to have her come for a visit. She didn't discuss the reason, but said she was taking a leave of absence from school for awhile. Judy packed while Mark waited in the living room. He had placed the backup tapes in a cardboard box and marked them "Mark Garrison—hold for evidence." There was no other identification on the box— nothing that would link them to the Archer affair. Mark was sure they would be safe in the evidence room at Riverside. He was struck by the thought that in this box was the formula for the remedy for all that was wrong with the human race. And it didn't escape his memory that the original disks were in someone else's hands. The more Mark invested himself in the Archer affair, the more he appreciated its consequences.

Judy set a large suitcase down at the door of her bedroom. When Mark took it to his car, he noticed that the black car was still across the street. "Do you know who's in that black car across the street?" he asked Judy.

Judy walked to the balcony window in the front of the townhouse. She looked down at the late model sedan parked across the street. Because the windows of the car were slightly tinted she couldn't identify the driver. "No, I don't," she said to Mark. "Why?"

"Nothing," said Mark, trying not to alarm Judy. "He was parked there when we came. I guess I'm just playing cop."

Judy packed another smaller suitcase and a hanging bag to carry on the airplane. Mark carried the suitcase and Judy carried the hanging bag. They loaded the baggage into Mark's unmarked police car. Judy went back into the house to take Kelly out on the leash, then showed Mark where Kelly's supplies were. He had agreed to pick up Kelly and his supplies on the way back from the airport. Although he hadn't had a dog since he was a child, he looked forward to keeping Kelly while Judy was away. As they pulled away from Judy's townhouse, Mark made a mental note of the license number on the black sedan.

Judy checked her bags at the curb and gave Mark a long goodbye kiss. "You have my parent's number, right? You'll call me?"

"Every day, Judy. Please let me know when you get there. I'm sure that the city police will have this thing wrapped up shortly. Please don't let anyone know where you are, okay?"

"I love you, Mark."

"I love you, Judy. We have a lot to talk about."

"We have a lifetime."

Neither wanted to let go of the other. Mark was the first to pull away. He got in his car as Judy entered the terminal. All the way to Judy's townhouse, he played over and over in his mind how he would ask her to marry him. He knew that it was too soon after Bob's suicide. Judy would have to set the pace.

The black car was gone when Mark pulled up in front of Judy's townhouse. He was surprised when Kelly didn't meet him at the door. Stepping into the townhouse, he called her name, but there was no response. When he turned from the foyer into the living room, he saw Kelly lying in the middle of the room. There were bloodstains under her mouth, but she was breathing. The house was trashed. Mark called 911. As soon as the police arrived, Mark took Kelly to his veterinarian. The doctor agreed to call after he had examined the dog.

By the time Mark returned to the townhouse, the police had dusted the townhouse doors for prints and were gone. There was black powder everywhere. A note was left behind asking Mark to contact the city police. He decided not to say anything to Judy until after he had cleaned the townhouse.

After several hours of straightening up, the phone rang. Kelly had received a blow to the ribs, probably from a kick. Several ribs were broken and there was evidence of internal bruising, but he would probably recover. The veterinarian wanted to keep him overnight for observation. He would call again the next day if Kelly could be taken home. Mark was relieved.

Mark called Sue and told her that he would be taking a day of personal leave. He gave her Judy's number in case he needed to be reached. It would take at least a full day to clean up the apartment and put Judy's things away. When he got to his own place, his answering machine was flashing. Judy had arrived safely. He decided not to call her until tomorrow. He wasn't a very good actor. She would detect that something was wrong.

Tomorrow, Mark would go to the city police department to get caught up on Bev's death and the burglary at Judy's, then he would go back to the townhouse. He remembered the black sedan in front of Judy's and called Louise Gordon. After giving her a description and the license number, he sat down in front of the television set with a nuked TV dinner. Bev's murder was still in the news. Police were confident that they could solve the killing. Mark would get the details tomorrow.

Judy unpacked her things in the same bedroom where she grew up. It would be the first night that she had stayed in that room since she left home after high school. So many memories were flooding into her mind that for awhile she was able to forget about Bob, Mark, Bev, Scott Dressler, and all the rest. It was comforting to return to earlier times—times when life was simpler and more promising. Maybe she and Mark could rediscover life on simpler terms. She looked forward to his phone call.

Billy Hudson learned about Bev's death from the television news. He was in the rec room on his tier. Bev's body was removed from her apartment before the press arrived, so Billy was spared seeing pictures of Bev tied to a chair in her kitchen with her throat cut; nevertheless, he lost control. The rec room went silent when the news was reported. Everyone turned to watch Billy Hudson. He had a reputation for being unpredictable. Billy came to his feet, then hurled his chair into the TV set. The TV exploded and went silent. Prisoners between Billy and the TV had scattered. Guards came from every direction. They restrained Billy and took him to lockup. He lost his honor privileges and was moved off of the honor tier for ninety days. Nothing was noted on his record, however. Billy would never be the same after losing the only family member that still loved and supported him.

There was only one pawnshop in Bloomington. According to regulation the proprietor was required to send a monthly register of all items pawned for more than $100 to the Bloomington police. The register was then scanned by a police clerk and compared to a statewide listing of stolen goods on the computer. Processing the list was not a high priority at the Bloomington police department. It took over a month for the police to scan the report that included a central processing unit and filebox full of Zip disks pawned by a Wayne Burroughs. There was no match. No computer with that serial number had been reported missing.

According to the shop's written rules, if pawned items were not redeemed within thirty days, they belonged to the store. The owner was interested in the central processing unit. It was newer than the CPU that he used in the store. He asked his nephew to check it out. By the end of the thirty-first day, the CPU had been reformatted and placed in service at the pawnshop. Since the proprietor did not own a Zip drive, he had his nephew reformat the disks, which were than placed for sale. Several had already been sold.

Wayne Burroughs was still living at the boarding house, but his girlfriend had split. Burroughs was working at a sawmill as a material handler and had not run afoul of Sandra Johnson, his parole officer. He was restless, however, and could not get Harley out of his mind. Whatever was in the envelopes he had passed to Harley had changed Harley completely. Burroughs had found nothing at Billy Hudson's sister's place except the computer and the disks with Dr. Archer's name on them, but he didn't know what to do with the CPU so he pawned it. Then he read in the paper about Billy Hudson's sister. If they connected him to the burglary, he might be accused of the murder. He decided to redeem the computer and the disks.

Burroughs watched the pawnshop from across the street until he was sure no one was in the shop. He handed his pawn ticket to the proprietor. "Can't help you, sir," said the proprietor. "Anything left over thirty days becomes the property of the shop."

"You don't understand. I need the computer and the disks," Burroughs said with a glare.

The shopkeeper saw desperation in Burroughs' face and positioned himself behind the counter so that he could reach his silent alarm. "The computer is already in use and the disks have been reformatted. Some have been sold. There is nothing that I can do for you, sir. Sorry."

Burroughs reached for the shopkeeper, but before he could grab him, the silent alarm had been pushed. From the corner of his eyes, Burroughs saw a red light begin flashing in the window of the store and realized what had happened. He left the store before the police arrived.

Two Bloomington officers arrested Burroughs at his boarding house, the address on the pawn records. He was putting clothes in a backpack. The same afternoon, he was arraigned for attempted assault and parole violation. Sandra Johnson arranged for the assault charge to be dropped and had Burroughs returned to R.C.I. on the parole violation.

It wasn't long before the word got out at R.C.I. that Wayne Burroughs was back. Hudson was still in lockup when Burroughs arrived at the prison. Because he and Billy Hudson had gotten along well as cellmates, Burroughs' case worker agreed to place them together as soon as Hudson was put back on the floor. Billy Hudson accepted the news gladly. He had no idea that Wayne Burroughs had burgled his late sister's apartment.

The black sedan was registered to a Chicago livery service. Records showed that the sedan was rented by a Tony Bock and was not due to be returned for several days. The address on the rental contract was phony. A bulletin was issued to all city precincts to be on the lookout for the sedan.

Mark was certain that before Bev was killed she had told her killer about the second set of disks. Why else would Judy's townhouse have been searched? He was surprised when Sue told him that Scott Dressler was on the phone. Except for seeing Dressler at Bob Archer's funeral, he didn't know Dressler, but his breach of confidence notwithstanding, Judy had spoken well of him on several occasions.

"Sergeant Garrison?" Dressler inquired.

"Yes."

"Hope I didn't disturb you, but I need to get in touch with Judy Archer. I've called her place repeatedly and no one answers or returns my messages."

"Why did you call me?"

"I'm afraid that something may have happened to her. She and Bev Hudson were friends. I know what's happened to Bev and I'm afraid for Judy." He sounded genuinely alarmed.

"Are you calling from your church, Pastor?"

"Yes."

"I'll come by in about an hour," Mark promised.

"Thank you."

Mark knocked on the door marked "Pastor's Office." He was shocked when Dressler opened the door. The side of Dressler's jaw looked like he had run into a building. "What happened to you?" he asked.

"I'd rather not say," Dressler responded.

"I think you should tell me," Mark said with a police voice.

"A man came into the office several days ago asking me about Judy Archer. I told him that I don't give out information about my members. The next thing I knew I was on the floor and he was standing over me with a closed fist. He searched my desk until he found the Church Directory, then grabbed it and left. I was just glad to be alive. I tried to reach Judy, but got no response."

"Judy is gone for awhile. Did you call the police?"

"No. I should have, but I was concerned about how it would look if it got into the papers, and how my congregation would react, especially if it became known that I had violated a confidence of Judy's"

Mark got a description of the man from Scott. "Did you see what kind of car he was driving?"

"No, it happened very quickly. But there was a black car parked in front of the church the last time Judy came to see me. When I approached it, the driver pulled away."

Mark drove to the city precinct in charge of the Hudson murder. Louise Gordon remembered Mark. "How is the jaywalking problem in the suburbs?"

He took a pass at her jibe. "There are some things that you may not know about the Hudson case that would be of help to you. Do you have a minute?"

"Come in." Louise pushed into her office ahead of Mark and sat down at her desk. "Sit down. What do you know about the Hudson case that we don't know?" she asked, implying that it could not be significant if it came from a small-town police department.

Again, Mark took a pass. "A month before Bev Hudson was murdered, her apartment was burgled. The burglary wasn't reported because her employer's property was stolen and they chose not to report the theft." Mark did not intend to name or implicate Bio-Gen. "Neither the burglar or the stolen items have been found, to my knowledge, but the burglary and the murder are connected."

"How so?"

Mark told Captain Gordon about Bob Archer's suicide and the research disks. He was vague about the project and made no mention of Harley and Barbara Arnold. He also told her about the assault on Scott Dressler.

"Why haven't you come forward about these matters, Sergeant Garrison. I could charge you with impeding an investigation, you know."

He thought that she would probably like nothing more. "I have just put the pieces together, myself, Captain." Mark was telling the truth. What he didn't tell her was that he had a duplicate set of research disks.

"I now have four felonies involving Dr. Archer—two burglaries, a murder, and an assault. Is there anything else you haven't told me?"

"Yes. I reported seeing a black sedan outside of Judy Archer's townhouse just before the burglary there. Pastor Dressler may have seen that same sedan at a time when Judy Archer was visiting his office. It drove off when he approached. I think that it may be a connecting link. Have you located it?"

"No. We have a bulletin out on the car, and the rental agency has been instructed to notify us if it is returned. We do have the identification of the driver, however. His name is Tony Bock. He has a sheet including two assaults. Both dealt down to misdemeanors."

"Why hasn't he been picked up?"

"No local address. The one he gave to the rental agency is an empty field."

"I'm personally interested in this case, Captain. May I call for an update from time to time?"

"Off the record?"

"Off the record."

"Sure."

"Thanks." Mark left Captain Gordon's office and drove to Judy's apartment to take care of Kelly. The dog was still in pain, but when Mark attached the leash to his collar, he was able to get to his feet and walk slowly to the front door. Mark carried him down the steps to the sidewalk and he did his business at the curb. He whined in the process, suggesting some internal pain. Mark carried him up the steps and set him down in the foyer. The dog followed Mark into the kitchen and watched Mark as he filled his bowl with dry food and poured water into his water bowl. Without eating or drinking, the dog lay down on the living room rug.

There were two messages on Judy's answering machine, both old messages from Scott Dressler. He picked up the phone and dialed Judy. It was probably time to tell her about the burglary at her place and the assault on Dressler.

"I know that you don't know what is missing, Mark, but how much damage was done?" Judy asked.

"One drawer is damaged and there's a knick on the coffee table in the living room. Otherwise, the apartment looks like it did when you left it."

Judy was deeply grateful to Mark for taking care of the apartment and Kelly. "I suppose they were after the disks," she speculated.

"Everything else seems untouched, Judy. Your jewelry is still upstairs, and your electronic equipment is intact, as far as I can tell."

"Are the tapes in Riverside?" she asked.

"Yes, in the evidence lockup at the police department."

"Should I come home? How is Pastor Dressler?"

"No, and okay. I have talked to the city police. There are no leads on the murder, the burglary at your place, or the assault on Dressler. All of it seems to be connected with someone in a black sedan. The police are looking for the car. How are you doing?"

"It's good to be with my parents, but I miss you Mark, and I'm getting bored."

"I miss you, Judy. I'm sure it won't be much longer."

19
The Team

After the aborted bio-ethics conference, David Daniel and his team returned to Little Rock. Daniel's opulent home was also the site of his recording studio. Every midday he and various guests sent a prayer and healing program to cable companies all across the nation. Handsome and charismatic in appearance, Daniel bilked millions of viewers out of their hard-earned money on the pretense of spreading the Word. The only word Daniel was interested in spreading was "give." His healing message was a combination of scripture and alternative medicine.

Sitting on the side of his swimming pool, Daniel met with his team—his business agent, Jimmy Fortin, and his public relations manager, Hulk Hoerber, men Daniel had known since childhood. The conversation was about the missing disks.

Fortin was a high school dropout with a history of run-ins with the Little Rock police. Hoerber was a high school football player who attended college on an athletic scholarship, but dropped out as part of an agreement following a gambling scandal. Both profited from Daniel's pseudo-ministry. David Daniel graduated from a Bible college and was ordained by a small Pentecostal church in Alabama. He made substantial offerings to the Pastor who ordained him. The Pastor's church, however, never seemed to benefit from their patron's generosity.

"Where's Murphy?" Fortin asked Daniel.

"How would I know? He hasn't been on time for an appointment for as long as I've known him. Supposedly, he's in town. His flight arrived last night."

Gene Murphy, a.k.a. Tony Bock, was a local hoodlum. Like the others, Murphy grew up with Daniel. David Daniel had used Murphy on other occasions as a bodyguard and as a pimp for his liaisons.

Daniel's houseman and security officer called on the two-way radio to announce the arrival of Murphy. "Buzz him in," Daniel instructed.

Murphy looked like a bouncer. He had broad shoulders, a thick muscular neck, and short dark hair. A scar divided his left cheek. He was average in height. "Sorry I'm late," he offered as he pulled up a deck chair and joined the team.

Daniel poured him a glass of iced tea with a lemon twist. "Bring us up to speed on the Archer business," he said.

"I ran into some problems," Murphy confessed. "The scientist is not going to be a problem for us. The police don't know anything about the research disks that were stolen from her place. Apparently no one reported the theft, so I don't know where to begin looking for them. But get this—there is another set of disks. Archer's wife has a backup set."

"I want both sets," Daniel demanded. "Unless we kill this project, the money tree dies."

"Mrs. Archer and her disks are gone. I checked out her place. There's nothing there."

"It will be worth your while to find her. And find both sets of disks."

Daniel dismissed Murphy with the wave of his hand. He then pulled a beach towel from around his shoulders and dove into his pool. Fortin and Hoerber got the message and left.

Murphy had parked the rented sedan at the airport. He hadn't expected Daniel to send him back to Chicago. Rather than go through the hassle of renting another car and using another I.D., he decided to use the same black sedan. What he didn't know was that the sedan had been reported to the city police by airport security. Captain Louise Gordon had ordered airport security to detain the vehicle if the driver attempted to exit the parking lot. As he approached the exit booth, Murphy saw a marked security vehicle pull in front of the gate. Leaving the car, he ran back toward the airport terminal. Out of shape and tired from traveling, Murphy was caught easily and taken into custody.

A veteran criminal, Murphy demanded a lawyer, but his first call was to David Daniel. Murphy was told to keep quiet until Daniel's lawyer could get to Chicago. Scott Dressler picked him out of a lineup as the man who beat him up. Louis Gordon had him held in the city lockup until the following morning on a charge of assault and auto theft.

It didn't take much to convince Gordon that Murphy was the man she was looking for in the burglary of Judy Archer's townhouse, the assault on Dressler, and the killing of Bev Hudson. All she had to do was prove it. His black sedan had been seen at the church and townhouse. A match of his DNA with traces of skin and blood found on Bev Hudson's face would be enough to charge him with murder. Murphy's attorney refused to let him be sampled for DNA, but the Assistant District Attorney got a court order for the test and it was only a matter of a day before the match was made. Gordon had Murphy dead to rights. He was charged with murder, burglary, assault, and auto theft.

Assistant District Attorney Pearl Black had known Bev Hudson. Pearl was a Master swimmer who trained with Bev for years. She did not reveal her friendship with Bev for fear that she would be asked to recuse herself. Black wanted nothing more than to see that justice was done in the brutal murder of her friend. "You are going away for a long time, then you're going to get an injection that will shut your miserable body down forever," Pearl told Murphy. He squirmed. He didn't like what he saw in her eyes.

"You can't threaten my client," Daniel's attorney objected.

"I want him to tell me who he is working for and the motive for his reign of terror."

"What's in it for him?" the attorney bargained.

"It depends on whether he says the right things."

"We want the death sentence off the table."

"Let's see what he has to say."

Gene Murphy spilled his guts. He implicated David Daniel and his team. All he could give them on the motive was that Daniel wanted Dr. Archer's research disks. He did not have the big picture.

Louise Gordon called the Little Rock police and had Daniel and his team taken into custody on the charge of conspiring to kill Bev Hudson. Daniel's attorney flew back to Little Rock to block the extradition of his clients. He was unsuccessful. Marshals escorted the whole bunch to Chicago where they were charged with conspiracy to commit murder.

20
Cellmates

After several weeks with her parents, Judy Archer was eager to go home. Mark called daily as he promised. He wasn't normally a talkative person, but with Judy things were different. Their conversations sometimes stretched to an hour or more. He had never felt so at ease with a woman before he met Judy. He was eager to share the news with her. Louise Gordon and Mark had become friends and Louise kept Mark informed as she promised. Although the Daniel team had not yet been convicted, they had been charged and they were being held without bail until the trial. Judy would be safe at home as long as the Daniel team was locked up. "I think it's safe for you to come home now," Mark said to Judy.

"Do you think they'll convict Daniel?" Judy asked.

"I have no doubt that the whole bunch will go away for a long time. The traces of blood and skin on Bev's face matched Gene Murphy, according to DNA testing. He implicated Daniel and his advisors, plus we have the business with the car and so on. I'm sure it will stick. So is Captain Gordon."

"What shall we do with the disks, Mark?" Judy asked, thinking that as long as the disks existed the matter was unresolved.

"We need to discuss that. For now, they're safe in the evidence cage at Riverside."

"Will you meet me at the airport?"

"What do you think?"

"I'll let you know my arrival time."

Mark hung his "police business" sign on the rear view mirror of his unmarked vehicle and parked in front of the arrival curb. He met Judy at the baggage pickup carousel dressed in civilian clothes. Judy was dressed casually in jeans and a sleeveless tee shirt. As soon as Judy departed from the escalator and began walking toward the carousel, Mark saw her. They both tried to restrain their pace, then locked in a hug that both wished would last forever. Arm in arm they watched the luggage parade in front of them until Judy's bags passed

135

by. Mark grabbed the suitcases and Judy grabbed her carryon.

"You look rested. Time with your parents was good for you," Mark remarked during the drive to Judy's townhouse.

"I didn't really rest until I read about the arrests. This whole thing has been very unsettling. My parents loved Bob and talked about him continuously. It was difficult for me. So much has changed. I'm glad to be home, Mark."

Mark took Kelly out on the leash while Judy took her carryon into the townhouse. She didn't know what to expect. Amazingly, the townhouse looked very much as she had left it. Some things were out of place, but Mark had done a great job. Kelly was excited to see Judy. Painfully, he put his front paws on Judy's legs. Judy got down on the carpeting and, leaning back against the couch, she sat with Kelly's head in her lap stroking the recovering dog.

After taking Judy's suitcases to her bedroom, Mark joined her and the dog. He sat on the couch.

"How bad was the apartment?" Judy asked.

Mark pointed out the dent in the coffee table. Apparently something had fallen on it. It was fixable. "There was fingerprint dust on the doors. I scrubbed them. Things were out of place. I put away what was obvious. There are some clothes on your bed. I wasn't sure where they belonged. Otherwise, there should be no surprises."

"Thanks." She leaned back and rested her head on Mark's leg. He bent forward and kissed her forehead.

"I've got to get back to work. I'll let you get settled in. Will you be all right by yourself?"

"I'll be fine."

Mark drove to the station in Riverside. He couldn't get his mind off of the disks in the evidence lockup. Obviously, they couldn't remain in Riverside much longer. The evidence lockup was inventoried every month. Someone would ask questions. He and Judy would have to make a decision soon. Since the church was most at risk if the disks were discovered, he would also include Scott Dressler in the discussion.

Billy Hudson was returned to his cell early. His time in lockup was reduced on the appeal of his caseworker who agreed that Hudson's meager prison wages would be withheld until the rec room television set had been replaced. This would put Hudson in an indigent status indefinitely. By prison rules, he could not return to work for thirty days after release from lockup, then his wages would be withheld for one year, meaning that personal needs and clothing would be issued by the state. He could appeal to friends and family, but with Bev dead there was no one who would send money to Billy. He was not a happy camper.

Wayne Burroughs had already been assigned to Hudson's cell. The prison cells were built to house one prisoner, but with the public clamoring for incarceration each cell had double occupants. The only exceptions to doubling were prisoners with physical handicaps and those in protective custody. The cells were 10 x 12 feet in size. Each contained stacked bunks, an open toilet, and a sink. Prisoners were each allowed a radio, TV, and eight books, meaning that two radios and two TV's could be operating at the same time in a room not much larger than a master bathroom. There was no "lights out" time in the tiers except for the infirmary. Light sleepers were out of luck.

Wayne and Billy greeted each other with a handshake. They both had stories to tell. One story that Wayne Burroughs would not tell was that he had burgled Bev Hudson's apartment looking for Bob Archer's magic potion. He knew that if Billy learned about his assault on Bev's apartment, he would go ballistic. Wayne would have to tread carefully. Although he was glad to be sharing a cell with Billy Hudson, he wasn't sure the risk was worth it.

"I hear they caught the son-of-a-bitch who killed your sister, Billy," a prisoner said to Billy Hudson in the cafeteria. Conversation stopped at the table where Billy, Wayne Burroughs, and four other men were drinking burnt coffee and eating cereal with warm milk. Bananas were the fruit of the day, but these had softened and darkened and were mushy when peeled. Breakfast for Billy and Wayne was at 10:00 a.m. due to the limited cafeteria size. Lunch was at 3:00 p.m. and dinner was at 10:00 p.m. for their rotation.

No one would have mentioned Bev Hudson a week before, but Billy had calmed down. It was hard to ignore the topic since it had been on the news. David Daniel's arrest upset many followers in the prison's Pentecostal population. No mention was made in the media about the sin gene or the gene therapy. Even Daniel and his group were keeping that topic under wraps. It would only be a matter of time, however, before it became public knowledge.

"I'd like to get that Murphy bastard assigned to my cell," said Billy. "He'd have a terrible accident."

"He's got friends with money. He's going to keep this thing in appeals for a long time. I doubt he'll come to R.C.I.," offered Wayne Burroughs.

"He's nothing but a local punk from Little Rock, but with the backing of David Daniel, he'll get a good mouthpiece," another prisoner added.

"Unless Daniel rolls on him," suggested Burroughs. "And I wouldn't put that past him. Conspiracy isn't going to put Daniel away forever if he deals." It was likely that Daniel would deal with the prosecutors in order to get Murphy convicted and reduce his own sentence. If he didn't, certainly Fortin or Hoerber would. Murphy was the logical fall guy, and the person who fingered him first would get the best deal.

Another prisoner at the table said, "The guy deserves what he gets. The stupid jerk hit her with his bare fist and left skin and blood on her face. You would think he would have worn gloves."

Billy was on his feet before the sentence was finished. Wayne Burroughs grabbed him by the shirt and pulled him back to his chair. "Don't do it, Billy. You're on thin ice as it is." Billy sat down. The other prisoner left the table without taking his tray. Silence followed.

"The guy was right, Wayne," said Billy when the two returned to their cell. "This guy Murphy was as dumb as a stick. I can't think straight when I hear his name. Bev lived in a rough neighborhood. I told her a thousand times to get a piece and keep it loaded. She was a looker living alone in the city—a sitting duck."

"Being above a grocery store was a help," Burroughs said thoughtlessly. The minute he said it, he realized what he had done. His eyes darted to Billy to see if his stupid slip had been caught. Immediately he turned on his TV to divert the conversation.

Billy stood up and walked past Burroughs to the TV. He turned it off. Burroughs was sitting on the edge of his lower bunk with Billy standing over him. "How did you know that Bev lived over a grocery store?" he asked.

"You mentioned it, I think." Burroughs' voice was shaky and he was looking away from Billy.

"I would never have told you where Bev lived," Billy replied.

"I, I don't know how else I could have known it," Burroughs stammered.

Before the guards could get to Billy Hudson, he had beaten a confession out of Wayne Burroughs. His cellmate told him about the burglary of the disks, but convinced Billy that he had nothing to do with what happened to Bev afterwards. He was after the stuff that Billy was getting for Harley. Hudson believed him. If he hadn't he would have killed Burroughs. As it was, Burroughs would never recover from the damage Billy did to his face.

The beating at R.C.I. was printed in Riverside's weekly paper on the third page of the news section, although the details were sketchy. Mark's eyes were attracted to the name Billy Hudson. Billy's sentence had been extended for administering a severe beating to his cellmate when it was discovered that his cellmate had burgled Hudson's sister's apartment while on parole. Mark called Judy and told her about the article.

"That means that Wayne Burroughs, not Bio-Gen, has the original disks," Judy observed.

"You're right. There was nothing in the article about the disks or the CPU."

"I have many friends who are guards at R.C.I. I'll find out what happened to the disks," Mark promised.

Burroughs was in the infirmary recovering from the beating. His face had been stitched, but it was out of the question that plastic surgery would be offered. Prisoners received only basic medical care. He would bear the scars, off-center nose, and flattened cheekbone for the rest of his life. Actually, it put character into what was otherwise a lackluster face. A guard from Burroughs' tier stepped into the infirmary and asked the infirmary attendant to step out. He pulled the curtain around Burroughs' bed so that his "interview" would be private. "What did you take from Bev Hudson's apartment, Burroughs?" he asked.

"I don't know what you're talking about," Burroughs mumbled through swollen lips.

"How would you like me to lean on that cheekbone, Burroughs?"

"A computer and some disks, that's all."

"What did you do with them?"

"Pawned them in Bloomington."

The guard left the infirmary without touching Burroughs. He called Mark Garrison and told him where the disks were. "I owe you," Mark said.

"Next time we're on the river, you buy the bait."

"Done deal."

Riverside library had a collection of Illinois phone books. Mark located the only pawnshop in Bloomington and struck pay dirt. The disks had been reformatted and all of them had now been sold. The hard disk in the CPU had been low-formatted and was being used at the store.

Mark decided that it was time to talk to Judy and Scott.

Scott Dressler's face was in the last stage of healing. The side that Murphy hit was yellow. Dressler told his congregation that he had fallen in the yard. With Daniel and the others in custody, Dressler was trying to put the whole

Archer issue behind him. He had buried Bob Archer, officiated at a graveside committal for Bev Hudson, and betrayed Judy Archer. Because of him the whole religious community, including David Daniel and company, had learned about the Archer research. All Dressler wanted was to forget the whole thing and get back to pastoring his congregation, so when he heard Mark Garrison's voice on the other end of the phone, he was leery.

"Pastor, this is Sergeant Garrison of the Riverside Police Department."

"Yes, hello Sergeant. How can I help you?"

"I'd like to bring this Archer business to a conclusion, but I need to sit down with you and Judy Archer. When would be a good time for us to meet?"

"Does Judy Archer want to meet with me?" Dressler asked hopefully.

"I haven't talked with her yet, but I'm going to call her next. It's important that we meet."

"I'll be in my office most of tomorrow, especially in the morning. Can you come by then?"

"We'll be there around 9:30. If Judy can't make it for any reason, I'll call you. If you don't hear from me today, expect us tomorrow."

Scott wanted to ask about the topic of the meeting. He couldn't imagine that there was anything left to talk about except his breach of Judy's confidence, which he hoped to repair. It would be painful, to be sure.

"I don't have any desire to meet with Pastor Dressler," Judy said with finality. "It's because of him that Bev Hudson is dead. If he hadn't gotten David Daniel alarmed, Bev would be alive today."

"I don't think that's entirely fair, Judy. I'm sure that Bob's research would have surfaced with or without Dressler. He understood the impact the research could have on the church and he felt that it was necessary to discuss it with his professor for the greater good. It was Dr. Schmidt who convened the meeting of church leaders."

"Pastor Dressler should have told me what he was going to do. We could have warned Bev."

Mark convinced Judy to meet with Scott Dressler, who was waiting for them in his office at 9:30 as planned. Judy entered the office first and stepped to the side, not greeting or extending her hand to her Pastor. Mark and Scott shook hands. Judy waited for the Pastor to make the first move. He motioned for all of them to sit and offered coffee. Both Mark and Judy accepted and Dressler left the room.

"You have to talk to him, Judy."

"I know."

Dressler returned with a tray and each took a mug of black coffee. "Judy, I don't know where to start," Dressler began. "Perhaps I should start by saying that I am sorry I didn't tell you that I was going to speak with Dr. Schmidt about Dr. Archer's research." He didn't offer any explanation, but waited for Judy to respond.

"A lot has happened because of what you did."

"I realize that and I regret what has happened, but I must tell you, Judy, that the stakes were pretty high for the church and I felt compelled to get counseling. I never intended for it to be widely broadcast, at least not as quickly as it was. And who could have predicted David Daniel's behavior?"

"I accept your apology, Pastor," Judy said unconvincingly in an effort to move forward.

With some relief, Mark interjected, "There is another matter that needs to be discussed. It's the reason we're here."

Scott Dressler was relieved. He didn't expect Judy to return to his church, but at least they had buried the hatchet. "What's left to discuss?" Scott asked.

"The research tapes," Mark answered.

"The stolen tapes?" Scott said, curiously.

"The original disks were stolen from Bev Hudson's apartment, as we all know. I know who took them and what has happened to them. A former prisoner at R.C.I. who saw the effect that Dr. Archer's gene therapy had on a prisoner named Harley stole them. He wanted that therapy for himself. He thought he could find it at Bev Hudson's apartment. Instead he found disks with Dr. Archer's name on them and stole the disks and Bev's CPU. When he got them, he didn't know what to do with them so he pawned them at a Bloomington pawnshop. They have since been reformatted and sold. That record of Dr. Archer's sin gene therapy is gone, but there is another set of disks copied from the first."

Scott looked at Mark intently. "Where are the copied disks?"

"In a place where they're safe," Mark answered. Mark wasn't sure that Dressler could be trusted to keep the location confidential. "The reason that we're here is that a decision must be made as to what to do with them."

"Would you be willing to invite Dr. Schmidt to join us in this discussion?" Scott asked. He knew that Schmidt was still having discussions about the gene therapy with his confidential advisors.

"Not unless he's here in person. Would he be willing to come for a meeting?"

"Yes," Scott answered. "He is the only person I know that I would trust to give us advice that would cover all the bases."

"How soon could he be here?" Mark asked.

"I'll call him now and ask," Scott said as he reached for his desk phone.

It was arranged for Dr. Schmidt to meet with Mark, Judy, and Scott Dressler.

The two special committees formed by Dr. Gene Schmidt after the aborted bio-ethics conference had met with Schmidt again in his office at the seminary. The communications group was disbanded when the research group reported that there were no disks and therefore it would be unlikely that the gene therapy would be produced again. The research group, however, had met several times more. Their debate centered on the possibility and consequences of a new therapy. If Dr. Archer had done it once, what would be the odds that someone at Bio-Gen or another scientist could overcome the effects of the 15105 mutation?

Dr. Schmidt had joined these meetings. The debate was theoretical. No one knew of the copies made by Bev Hudson. Unlike David Daniel, whose exploitive healing ministry was threatened by the existence of a material that would cure the ills of humanity, the members of this committee took the high road. Their debate centered on whether the gene therapy was a providential gift or just another failed attempt on the part of humankind to do what was reserved for God. The camps were split and solid arguments were made for both points of view.

The first group compared the gene therapy to other advances in medical science that had the effect of slowing down the decline of the human body and extending life. Some discoveries had eliminated certain diseases altogether. Many of these advances had been made in spite of criticism and skepticism. In some cases, like Dr. Archer's, unauthorized research had been necessary. In time, however, the work had been validated and many lives improved or saved. This group supported the possibility that Dr. Archer was doing God-pleasing work and the result would be a fuller life for those who received his therapy. To this end, the church should stand in support of his findings and promote the continuation of his research.

The second group, on the other hand, likened the gene therapy discovery to other attempts of humans to be "like God." Knowing the depth of human depravity and the height of human pride, anyone who attempted to overcome the "sin gene" was playing God and would run afoul of his warnings against idolatry as stated in the First Commandment and the Great Shema. The single most important contribution of this group was the discovery that the 15105 gene had the imprint of God himself. One of the men on the research committee was a Hebrew scholar. He had reported to the group that the number 15105 was the alphanumeric spelling of the name God had claimed for himself at the burning bush, where he encountered Moses as reported in Exodus:

Then Moses said to God, "Indeed when I come to the children of Israel and say to them, 'The God of your fathers has sent me to you,' and they say to me 'What is his name?' what shall I say to them?"

And God said to Moses, "I AM WHO I AM." And he said, "Thus you shall say to the children of Israel, 'I AM has sent me to you.'"

The alphanumeric characters for I AM are 15105. It is statistically beyond coincidence that the very gene that is defective in all humankind, and that whose repair reverses the effects of sin predicted in the holy writings is imprinted with the name of God himself. For this reason, the second group refused to offer any congratulations to Dr. Archer, or any encouragement to continue his research on the grounds that he had treaded on holy ground and his work could only bring down the wrath of God.

Dr. Schmidt had his own agenda. He was a bio-ethicist of world renown. His specialty was the study of the ethical and moral implications of new biological discoveries and biomedical advances, as in the fields of genetic engineering and drug research. The ethical consequences of each group were significant. If the first group was right that Dr. Archer's project had providential origins, then there were ethical consequences by not pursuing it and making the therapy available to as many as possible. On the other hand, if the work was a "filthy rag" in the sight of God, because it would undo what had been done by God himself, to promote it would be an affront to people of faith.

It was in the midst of these debates that Scott Dressler's invitation came to Dr. Schmidt. "There is a new development in the Archer matter, Dr. Schmidt," Dressler began. "I believe that it would be to your advantage to meet with me and several others. Can you come?"

"Not at present. My schedule is pretty full, Scott. Can we schedule a telephone conference?"

Scott put the call on hold and asked Mark and Judy whether they would be willing to discuss the matter over the phone. They both declined. "It would be better if you were here. I believe it's important." Dressler was not willing to disclose the existence of the disk copies. He remembered only too well how Schmidt had over-reacted by canceling the Bio-Ethics in Religion Conference.

Dr. Schmidt agreed to come. He could not get a flight until tomorrow.

21
Schwinn

Mark was glad to have Judy back at her townhouse. They left Dressler's together and decided to take the rest of the day for themselves.

"Do you have a bike?" Judy asked.

"Somewhere," Mark answered. "Why?"

"Let's take a bike ride."

Mark hadn't been on his bike in years. He wasn't even sure where it was. They agreed to meet at the Riverside Park in two hours, which would give Mark time to find his bike and see whether it worked.

Judy was waiting with her mountain bike. She had spent a lot of money on a Gary Fisher Sugar-1 in Amarillo yellow. It was one of the few vices she allowed herself. The bike was a dream and when Judy was on it, she felt as though she was floating on air.

Mark's unmarked police car pulled up at the park with a bicycle wheel sticking out of the trunk. He pulled the bike out and got on. If she had been a police officer she would have given him a sobriety test. He was all over the sidewalk. She tried not to laugh when he rode up on his thirty-plus year old Schwinn Collegiate, also yellow. It was one stage removed from the old bicycles with the enormous front and tiny rear tires. The sprockets were caked with grease and dust from years of storage. The pencil-thin tires were stricken with dry rot. It was amazing that they hadn't burst when he inflated them.

Judy couldn't restrain herself. "Where did you get *that* relic of the fifties?" she asked.

Mark ignored the slur. He was chagrined when he saw Judy's mountain bike. She took them on an easy ride around the lake, not getting too far from Mark's car in case of Schwinn-failure.

Judy had packed a tablecloth and some sandwiches. They spread the tablecloth on the ground and ate lunch. Mark's calves were tight and his butt was sore from riding on the narrow seat. Judy felt great. "I missed you when I was at my parent's house. I didn't expect that I would miss you as much as I did."

"We need to talk about what's going on with us, Judy."

144

"I agree, but I'm feeling some guilt about the feelings I have, especially this soon after Bob's death."

"I understand, but what's gained by putting off our feelings for each other?"

"I really don't know, Mark. That's part of what's bothering me."

Mark lay back on the tablecloth and put his hands under his head for a pillow. Judy lay back alongside him and slid next to him. He moved slightly away. There was no one around. It would have been easy to make love to Judy right there in the park, and he wanted nothing more. She excited him in her short shorts and flimsy blouse, but Mark was old-fashioned. He wanted to save this moment for their wedding night.

"Is there something wrong, Mark?" she asked when he slid away.

"Judy, I would love to hold you right now, but I'm not sure I could restrain myself. I want this to be right." He hoped she would understand. She slid next to him and pulled herself up on his chest. Their mouths met and they kissed. As quickly, Judy got up, folded the tablecloth, and they rode back to their cars.

"I love you, Mark. Everything will be right for us," she said as they left.

Scott Dressler met Dr. Schmidt at the airport. "Have you had breakfast?" he asked.

"No. They served juice and an English muffin, but I need to stop for something more," Schmidt replied.

Scott made a stop at Denny's on the way to his office. It brought back memories of his two encounters with Judy Archer and Bev Hudson. Both men ordered skillet specials. While they ate Schmidt brought Dressler up to date on the discussions taking place within the research committee. Dressler was pleased that the denominational leaders on the research committee were able to work together without territorial rancor. He attributed that to Gene Schmidt. Schmidt was a good negotiator and had been effective in some difficult bio-ethical debates in the past. Dressler was also pleased that the discussions had stayed focused on the greater good and that there had been no repeats of the Daniel type.

"Who are the people that we'll be meeting with this morning?" Schmidt asked.

"Judy Archer is the wife of Dr. Bob Archer. Sergeant Mark Garrison is with the Riverside Police Department. He investigated the Archer suicide and became a good friend of Mrs. Archer and Dr. Hudson, Archer's lab associate. After Dr. Hudson's murder, he stayed close to Mrs. Archer for reasons that will be explained later. They are fine people who are trying to get on with their lives."

"What is the issue that brought me here?"

Scott didn't want to discuss the existence of the disk copies until everyone was together. "They have information that will put new life into your research committee. Frankly, I'd like for them to be with us before we put the issue on the table."

Mark and Judy were parked in front of the church when the men arrived. Everyone was introduced on the sidewalk and the whole group settled into Pastor Dressler's office. The church secretary had not yet arrived, so Scott set up the coffee table. "Coffee will be ready in a few minutes," he announced.

While waiting for coffee, the conversation was light and introductory. "Pastor Dressler and I had breakfast on the way to the church," Schmidt said. "He told me a little about you, but perhaps we could each speak about our connection with Dr. Archer and his project."

His gaze was focused on Mark Garrison. Judy Archer's connection was obvious. He was more than a little curious about Mark's connection. Mark responded. "I investigated Dr. Archer's unfortunate death and came to be acquainted with Mrs. Archer and Dr. Hudson. Since Dr. Hudson's murder, I've been concerned about Mrs. Archer's safety. I've kept in touch with her and the case."

By the way Mark and Judy were relating to one another, Schmidt assumed that a friendship had developed. He was satisfied that Mark had no personal agenda other than the interests of Judy Archer. "And you, Mrs. Archer?"

"What are you asking, Dr. Schmidt?" Judy responded.

"Are you furthering your husband's work in some way?"

"No. I'm not a scientist. I'm a high school teacher. Bob didn't discuss his work at home. I've learned more about his work since he died than I did when we were married."

Dr. Schmidt was becoming more curious about the purpose of the meeting. "Scott, can we get to the purpose for this meeting. I have a late morning plane to catch and I'm not even certain why I'm here."

Dressler got up and walked to the coffee table. He took orders and poured coffee for all four. As he carried a tray into his office, he answered Schmidt's question, "There is a full set of disks containing Dr. Archer's work. It was copied from the originals."

Dr. Schmidt was silent. He watched Scott for a minute, then broke the silence. "Where are they now?" It was a logical, but unfortunate first question.

Mark interjected, "Where they are is not as important as what should be done with them." There was no way that Mark and Judy were going to disclose the whereabouts of the disks to Dressler and Schmidt until there was a plan for their future safekeeping.

It was obvious that Schmidt was going to have to bring Judy and Mark up to speed on the discussions taking place. "There are some church leaders discussing the possible use or disposition of the therapy discovered by Dr. Archer. On one side, they feel that what Dr. Archer has done advances human science to a new level and is not inconsistent with other medical science intended for the good of humankind. They feel that this development is providential. There are others who feel that it is an attempt to usurp God's historic plan for the salvation of believers."

Judy spoke for the first time. "My husband was not a believer. He was a scientist. His only objective would have been for the common good."

"I have no doubt that you're correct, Mrs. Archer," Schmidt replied. "I'm not judging his motives. His discovery is important either way and it has implications for everyone. My concern is that what was a theoretical debate has now become real. We are again faced with decisions with enormous consequences."

"One obvious alternative," said Mark, "is to dispose of the disks. No one outside of this room is aware of their existence."

"That is a possibility," agreed Schmidt, "but let's keep that on the back burner for now."

"Another possibility," said Dressler, "is to turn them over to Bio-Gen. They are the true owners. The work was done by their employee at their facility."

"Their work on the Human Genome Project would be in real jeopardy if it became known that unauthorized human trials were done by my husband," Judy added. "They might not be objective about continuing the work that Bob started."

"Folks, let's get an overview," Schmidt interjected. "Dr. Archer identified a common mutation in gene 15105, which, one of our committee members has made known, is the Hebrew alphanumeric equivalent to the name of God, I AM, as given to Moses in Exodus. This seems to be the alteration that God made to the human structure after the Fall. As a consequence we are no longer born in the image of God, but in the image of Adam—a distorted image of God. In the process of his work, Dr. Archer discovered a repair for the mutant gene, a way to replace the missing base pair in gene 15105. His human trials demonstrated that the repair works, but that the therapy cannot be withdrawn. Now we know that the protocol for developing the therapy is again accessible. We are at a historical crossroads. Does everyone understand the consequences of our decision here?"

Scott had had all he could take. He would not play God. "I think everyone understands the seriousness of the decision, Dr. Schmidt. There is more than Dr. Archer's project at stake here, however. We can't forget the reaction of David Daniel when his empire was threatened by Archer's gene therapy. If the project is continued and the therapy is made available, can you imagine the commercial greed that will be turned loose? I'm afraid that before the liposome therapy could change the basic nature of society, we would devour ourselves fighting for monopolies to research and produce it, then we would wait for a period of years to get it approved by the FDA. Once it was approved, the drug companies would price it out of the reach of most people in order to recover their research and development costs. Its distribution would be limited to those who have prescription insurance or could afford to buy it or get it in a foreign market. Because of its tremendous commercial value, it would be controlled by regulatory agencies of the federal government. It would never become an aspirin equivalent on the market place. If we allow these disks to be released we will be opening a can of worms. That's the practical side."

"There is another issue that's of greater importance to me," Dressler continued. "It has been presented by part of the research committee. It has to do with trespassing in God's territory. Dr. Archer happened on something of providential consequence, then killed himself. Why? He saw what happened to Harley and Barbara Arnold. Why didn't he use the liposome treatment himself instead of taking his own life? Dr. Archer was not a believer. Is that right, Judy?"

"I can't say who is a believer and who isn't. Bob was a scientist and a humanist. He never criticized my faith, but he didn't profess it, either."

"What would happen when an unbeliever or, giving Dr. Archer the benefit of neutrality, an agnostic, discovers something that defies scientific explanation? I believe that several things happened to Dr. Archer. First, I believe that he realized he had stumbled on hard evidence of the Fall. Then, I believe that he was overwhelmed when he discovered the remedy. He had to admit to things that he had never taken seriously. Second, I believe that because he made the mistake of doing human trials without authorization, he knew that his career with Bio-Gen was over and his chances of being taken seriously as a disciplined scientist were limited. All that combined with fatigue pushed him over the edge. His demise is a precursor of the demise of society if given access to this therapy. I opt to destroy the disks and let God work out the salvation of the world," Dressler concluded.

Mark was not a scientist. He knew that Pastor Dressler and Dr. Schmidt were light-years ahead of him academically and he was not on a level field with them, but he felt compelled to enter the conversation. "I've spent a lot of years dealing with the kinds of people that you will never meet—people like Harley and Barbara Arnold. Many have never had a chance at life. They're products of their upbringing and will never know compassion and love for others. They will never be free from the demons that possess them, literally. For a brief moment, Harley and Barbara Arnold experienced love. They rose above their circumstances. They had a better than even shot at life. Unfortunately, Dr. Archer's death ended their chances, but if his work is allowed to continue, others will benefit. I know that it is a self-serving world and people will exploit others in the process of developing this therapy, but I opt for releasing the disks to Bio-Gen or some other lab with the capability of continuing the project."

Judy was proud of Mark. She knew how difficult it was for him to speak up. She liked his compassion and concern for others. Without thinking, she reached for his hand, gave it a quick squeeze and released it. It was unnoticed by the others. Just when Scott Dressler had convinced her to destroy the disks, Mark persuaded her not to. It wasn't that she wasn't able to decide for herself, but that both sides of the issue were valid. Because there didn't seem to be a convincing option, she elected to remain silent.

Schmidt had an ethical bias. Right conduct was his objective in all things. Like Judy, he could accept valid, but conflicting options, although the choices were not the same as they were for Judy. For Schmidt, the choices were to see that, if continued, the research and development of the liposome therapy would benefit everyone who desired it, or that the belief system of billions of people would be honored and the disks would be destroyed. It was a matter of right conduct.

In the end, it was Judy who cast the deciding vote. "After listening to each of you, I suggest that the disks be destroyed and that their destruction be witnessed by all four of us so there will never be any doubt as to the outcome of Bob's project. If God wants this therapy, the destruction of the disks will not stop its development. If He doesn't, His own plan has given hope to countless people for centuries and will result in something far greater than we can imagine. I truly believe that. My husband was a thoughtful man whose goal in life was to advance the human cause. He wasn't bound by religious rules, and yet when confronted with religious truths, he took the wrong course. If Bob could be so corrupted by the possibilities of his work that he would violate the basic tenets of his discipline and then destroy his own life, what evil possibilities does this so-called remedy have for the rest of humankind? I believe that Pastor Dressler is right in doubting our ability to handle a cure for sin. I opt for leaving God's work with God."

"It's time for a decision," said Dr. Schmidt. "Since there are four of us in the room, I'm going to abstain from voting. This will give us a certain outcome. It seems to me that you, Scott, and you, Judy, would vote for destroying the disks. Is that correct?"

Both nodded in agreement.

"And you, Mark, would vote for continuing the research project. Is that correct?"

Mark nodded.

"If God has worked through Dr. Archer, let us all be forgiven. Let's get the disks and destroy them."

22
Trash-Raiders

"I know where the disks are," Mark said. "I'll go and get them. It will take me about forty-five minutes to drive to Riverside and back. Where shall I bring them?"

"I believe we should all go together," Scott said, not fully understanding the reason for his caution.

The four got into Mark's unmarked police car and rode with him to the Riverside Police Station. When Mark and his passengers arrived at the Riverside Police Department they followed Mark to his desk, passing Sue. Mark wanted to make a beeline to the evidence cage and withdraw the backup disks and leave before his entourage got the attention of Captain Myers.

Riverside was a small police department. There was no one individual in charge of the evidence in the lockup cage. Each officer stored what applied to his assigned case. Monthly the evidence was inventoried by Sue and recorded on an inventory form. She checked the container markings, case number, and number of containers. It was not her job to open the containers and visually inventory the contents.

Mark unlocked the evidence cage and went to the cabinet where he had stored the box containing the backup disks. The cabinet was empty. Mark looked into the cabinets alongside his. His box was not there. Judy, Pastor Dressler, and Dr. Schmidt were waiting for him in the break room. Fortunately, they could not see the look of panic on his face. He called Sue on the interoffice phone and asked her to come to the evidence lockup.

"What's up?" she asked as she approached Mark.

"Sue, I had a cardboard box in my cabinet in the lockup. It's not where I put it. Did you move a box from my cabinet?"

"I sure did. I inventoried the evidence cage yesterday. Your evidence was not properly marked so I put it on your desk so it could be logged in on the inventory. It should be on your desk, Mark."

Mark breathed a sigh of relief. "Sorry about that Sue. I stored it in a hurry. Guess I forgot procedure. Thanks." Mark did not want Sue to ask questions about the contents of the box. He headed straight for his desk. The break room was out of the line of vision of the evidence cage and Mark's desk so he was able to avoid being seen by Judy and the others. There was no box on his desk. Again, he called Sue. She had no answer for the missing box.

"I left the box in plain view, Mark. I have no idea where it went," she said.

"When did you put it on my desk?" Mark asked.

"Yesterday before I went home. About five."

"Who cleaned the station last night, Sue?" Mark asked.

"The usual crew," she answered.

"Will you get them on the phone, Sue?"

"I'll try. They work nights. It might be hard to find them during the day."

Mark went into the break room and sat down with Judy and the others. It was time to share his dilemma. "There is a complication," he confessed. "We're having difficulty locating the box containing the disks."

Mark was the only one of the group who had insisted on furthering Dr. Archer's project. He was alone with the disks. Scott didn't like what he was thinking. Did Mark intentionally misplace the disks while the others were in the break room? "How could this be?" he asked. "I thought the disks were safe." He hoped that his anxiety wasn't showing. Dr. Schmidt and Judy waited for Mark's reply.

"I stored the disks in a box in the lockup cage. Our department clerk inventoried the evidence yesterday and moved the box to my desk. Somehow the box was misplaced during the night. It's possible the cleaning crew moved it. We have a call in for them right now. I'm sure there is a reasonable explanation and that they will show up."

Before Mark could finish his weak explanation, Sue called him out of the break room. "I'm sorry, Mark, but the cleanup crew leader says that he thinks the box was discarded along with the cleanup trash. He's checking with the employee who cleaned your desk area. He'll get back to us."

"Find out who that is and where they can be reached. Let me know at once."

Mark wasn't usually this agitated, Sue thought. She felt responsible for his predicament and recalled the cleanup crew leader. There were two people assigned to the police department on the previous night—the crew leader and one other person, a service technician. Sue wrote down the name and phone number of the technician and gave the information to Mark.

As usual, the technician had placed the cleanup trash in a container behind the station. She had not seen any markings on the box and had disposed of it with several trash bags at the end of the evening. Mark walked to the rear of the building. He found a large green plastic container. It was empty. He didn't want to return to the break room.

"It seems as though the box containing the disks was discarded with the cleanup trash last night," Mark said to Judy.

"It's time for some good old-fashioned police work," Judy replied.

Mark agreed. He promised the group that he would do everything possible to locate the box. There was nothing else that could be done except to take Judy and Scott Dressler back to the church where Judy's car was parked. He offered to drive Dr. Schmidt to the airport. His offer was accepted. Before they left the police station, he promised to notify them at once when the disks were located. They authorized him to destroy the disks. Scott was uneasy about the sudden disappearance of the disks and the strange turn of events. He had no choice but to trust Mark.

After leaving the airport, Mark drove straight to the home of the service technician. She was certain that she remembered placing the box and two trash bags in the green container in the rear of the police station. She had no idea who was responsible for trash removal from there.

Sue informed Mark that the Riverside Municipal Haulers who were contracted by the city picked trash up twice weekly, then all trash was hauled to the county landfill. Mark called Ed Braun. "Ed, I need a favor," he began. He explained the situation to Ed without going into detail. He described the box and its markings, but not its contents. Ed was to speak with the driver and let Mark know the routine that they followed.

As usual, Ed was pleased to break out of his routine. He knew all of the city employees personally. The driver who had picked up trash at the Riverside Police Department remembered his pickup. There was no box. He distinctly remembered that the container was not facing the right direction for his truck to hoist it. He had to leave the truck, open the container, and remove two trash bags. This was unusual. Usually, the cleaning crew at the police station was pretty good about facing the container in the right direction. There was no box in the container or around the container. He dumped his truckload at the landfill. By now it would be buried.

There was nothing further for Mark to do. His investigation had come to a dead end. He believed the service technician and the hauler. Somewhere between the cleanup and the pickup the box had been lost or taken. Anyone could have gone through the trash behind the station during the night. It would explain the unusual position of the container. No one other than Mark or Judy knew the contents of the box. To a trash thief, the file box full of disks would have little value. Someone looking for those particular disks could change history.

Mark called Judy. "I've reached a dead end," he said. "The disks are lost or stolen. I don't know which. I'll contact your Pastor and Dr. Schmidt. I hope I haven't let you down, Judy."

There was nothing for Mark to do but to tell Scott Dressler the truth. Through a series of errors the disks were missing. Mark took full responsibility. He had intentionally been vague when he marked the cardboard box in which they were stored. That caused the clerk to place them on his desk for proper identification. She had erred by leaving the box outside of the lockup cage. Then the cleaning crew had mistaken it for trash and placed it in a trash container outside the building. That was the last time the box containing the backup disks had been seen. It was likely that the box had been taken by a trash can raider and that, finding the contents to be of little apparent value, he or she had disposed of them. Mark had no leads to follow.

Scott was convinced that Mark was telling the truth. He agreed to explain the situation to Dr. Schmidt. The whereabouts of the backup disks would have to remain a mystery for the moment.

The one man in Riverside who would know the local trash can raiders was Ed Braun. Ed agreed to tap the grapevine for any information regarding the missing box.

Mark felt as though he had failed Judy. "I talked with Pastor Dressler," Mark said to Judy on the phone. "He agreed to inform Dr. Schmidt that the disks are lost, probably stolen."

"What was his reaction?" she asked.

"Naturally, he would have preferred to see them destroyed, but there is nothing that anyone can do until or if they show up."

"Does this leave Bob's project open-ended?" she asked.

"Dr. Archer's project will always be open-ended. There's nothing to keep another scientist from making the same discovery that he made. Scientists all over the world are exploring the human genome. The 'sin gene' as Dr. Archer called it is there for someone to discover. Not to minimize Dr. Archer's work, but if he was able to find a therapy which could reverse its effect, there is nothing to keep another scientist from doing it, too. In that sense, the project is open-ended."

Mark was able to reduce things to their simplest terms. It was one of the qualities that Judy liked about him. "Would you like to have dinner with me tonight, Mark?"

"Yes, I would." He hoped she would want to get together, especially after his failure with the disks.

"Come at 7:00. I'll make meatloaf."

Mark came bearing gifts. In one hand he carried a bottle of champagne. In the other a box of Fannie Mae candy. "These are peace offerings," he said as he handed the packages to Judy at the door. Kelly was his old self and greeted Mark with a wag of his tail. Judy greeted Mark with a kiss.

"You don't need peace offerings," Judy assured him. "What happened with the disks was a series of unfortunate mistakes. We'll have to let it go. In fact, I'm ready to let the entire matter go. I hope you are."

"Judy, I'd rather talk about us."

"There's time for that. The meatloaf will be ready in about half an hour. Please pour some champagne while I put on a Johnny Mathis CD."

Mark popped the cork on the champagne bottle and poured two glasses. The music was already playing when he entered the living room. Judy was standing between Mark and an antique floor lamp. Mark could see the outline of Judy's body through her blouse. She was not wearing anything under her blouse. Her breasts were perfectly shaped. She had slipped out of her shoes and approached Mark in a dance position. He took her in his arms and danced her to the floor lamp, which he switched off. The only light in the room was the light coming out of the kitchen. They wrapped their arms around each other and swayed to *Chances Are*. All thoughts of Dr. Archer's project were quickly forgotten. Judy and Mark were one person in body, mind, and spirit. "It's time for us to talk about our future," Mark breathed into her ear.

"Yes, I will," Judy said, her mouth brushing against Mark's.

Mark put his hands on the side of her shoulders and pushed her back slightly so that he could look straight into her face. "Does that mean what I think it means?" he asked.

"Yes, it does," she said smiling.

"Does it mean that you'll marry me?" he asked, not yet believing what he had heard.

"Yes, it does," she said, still smiling.

Mark hadn't intended to go that far this soon. "I don't have a ring. I was going to go a little slower."

"Does that mean that you don't want to marry me, Mark?"

He held her so tightly she had to push back to get air. "As soon as possible."

"We'll talk to Pastor Dressler tomorrow," she said. As if to ring approval, the timer on the oven signaled that the meatloaf was ready.

Printed in the United States
6885